In the High Valley

Susan Coolidge

CHAPTER ONE : ALONG THE NORTH DEVON COAST

It was a morning of late May, and the sunshine, though rather watery, after the fashion of South-of-England suns, was real sunshine still, and glinted and glittered bravely on the dew-soaked fields about Copplestone Grange.This was an ancient house of red brick, dating back to the last half of the sixteenth century, and still bearing testimony in its sturdy bulk to the honest and durable work put upon it by its builders. Not a joist had bent, not a girder started in the long course of its two hundred and odd years of life. The brickwork of its twisted chimney-stacks was intact, and the stone carving over its doorways and window frames; only the immense growth of the ivy on its side walls attested to its age. It takes longer to build ivy five feet thick than many castles, and though new masonry by trick and artifice may be made to look like old, there is no secret known to man by which a plant or tree can be induced to simulate an antiquity which does not rightfully belong to it. Innumerable sparrows and tom-tits had built in the thick mats of the old ivy, and their cries and twitters blended in shrill and happy chorus as they flew in and out of their nests.

The Grange had been a place of importance in Queen Elizabeth's time, as the home of an old Devon family which was finally run out and extinguished. It was now little more than a superior sort of farmhouse. The broad acres of meadow and pleasaunce and woodland which had given it consequence in former days had been gradually parted with, as misfortunes and losses came to its original owners. The woods had been felled, the pleasure grounds now made part of other people's farms, and the once wide domain had contracted, until the ancient house stood with only a few acres about it, and wore something the air of an old-time belle who has been forcibly divested of her ample farthingale and hooped petticoat, and made to wear the scant kirtle of a village maid.

Orchards of pear and apple flanked the building to east and west. Behind was a field or two crowning a little upland where sedate cows fed demurely; and in front, toward the south, which was the side of entrance, lay a narrow walled garden, with box-bordered beds full of early flowers, mimulus, sweet-peas, mignonette, stock, gillies, and blush and damask roses, carefully tended and making a blaze of colour on the face of the bright morning. The whole front of the house was draped with a luxuriant vine of Gloire de Dijon, whose long, pink-yellow buds and cream-flushed cups sent wafts of delicate sweetness with every puff of wind.

Seventy years before the May morning of which we write, Copplestone Grange had fallen at public sale to Edward Young, a well-to-do banker of Bideford. He was a descendant in direct line of that valiant Young who, together with his fellow-seaman Prowse, undertook the dangerous task of steering down and igniting the seven fire-ships which sent the Spanish armada 'lumbering off' to sea, and saved England for Queen Elizabeth and the Protestant succession.Edward Young lived twenty years in peace and honour to enjoy his purchase, and his oldest son James now reigned in his stead, having reared within the old walls a numerous brood of sons and daughters, now scattered over the surface of the world in general, after the sturdy British fashion, till only three or four remained at home, waiting their turn to fly.

One of these now stood at the gate. It was Imogen Young, oldest but one of the four daughters. She was evidently waiting for someone, and waiting rather impatiently.

'We shall certainly be late,' she said aloud, 'and it's quite too bad of Lion.' Then, glancing at the little silver watch in her belt, she began to call, 'Lion! Lionel! Oh, Lion! Do make haste! It's gone twenty past, and we shall never be there in time.'

'Coming,' shouted a voice from an upper window; 'I'm just washing my hands. Coming in a jiffy, Moggy.'

'Jiffy!' murmured Imogen. 'How very American Lion has got to be. He's always "guessing" and "calculating" and "reckoning". It seems as if he did it on purpose to startle and annoy me. I suppose one has got to get used to it if you're over there, but really it's beastly bad form, and I shall keep on telling Lion so.'

She was not a pretty girl, but neither was she an ill-looking one. Neither tall nor very slender, her vigorous little figure had still a certain charm of trim erectness and youthful grace, though Imogen was twenty-four, and considered herself very staid and grown-up. A fresh, rosy skin, beautiful hair of a warm chestnut colour, with a natural wave in it, and clear, honest, blue eyes, went far to atone for a thick nose, a wide mouth, and front teeth which projected slightly and seemed a size too large for the face to which they belonged. Her dress did nothing to assist her looks. It was woollen, of an unbecoming shade of yellowish grey; it fitted badly, and the complicated loops and hitches of the skirt bespoke a fashion some time since passed by among those who were particular as to such matters. The effect was not assisted by a pork-pie hat of black straw trimmed with green feathers, a pink ribbon from which depended a silver locket, a belt of deep magenta-red, yellow gloves, and an umbrella bright navy-blue in tint. She had over her arm a purplish waterproof, and her thick, solid boots could defy the mud of her native shire.

'Lion! Lion!' she called again; and this time a tall young fellow responded, running rapidly down the path to join her. He was two years her junior, vigorous, alert, and boyish, with a fresh skin, and tawny, waving hair like her own.

'How long you have been!' she cried reproachfully.

'Grieved to have kept you, Miss,' was the reply. 'You see, things went contrary-like. The grease got all over me when I was cleaning the guns, and cold water wouldn't take it off, and that old Saunders took his time about bringing the can of hot, till at last I rushed down and fetched it up myself from the copper. You should have seen Cook's face! "Fancy, Master Lionel," says she, "coming yourself for 'ot water!" I tell you, Moggy, Saunders is past his usefulness. He's a regular duffer—a gump.'

3

'There's another American expression. Saunders is a most respectable man, I'm sure, and has been in the family thirty-one years. Of course he has a good deal to do just now, with the packing and all. Now Lion, we shall have to walk smartly if we're to get there at half-after.'

'All right. Here goes for a spin, then.'

The brother and sister walked rapidly on down the winding road, in the half-shadow of the bordering hedges. Real Devonshire hedgerows they were, than which are none lovelier in England, rising eight and ten feet overhead on either side, and topped with delicate, flickering birch and ash boughs blowing in the fresh wind. Below were thick growths of hawthorn, white and pink, and wild white roses in full flower interspersed with maple tips as red as blood, the whole interlaced and held together with thick withes and tangles of ivy, briony, and travellers' joy. Beneath them the ground was Strewn with flowers—violets, and king-cups, poppies, red campions, and blue iris—while tall spikes of rose-coloured foxgloves rose from among ranks of massed ferns, brake, hart's tongue, and maiden's-hair, with here and there a splendid growth of Osmund Royal.

To sight and smell, the hedgerows were equally delightful.Copplestone Grange stood three miles west of Bideford, and the house to which the Youngs were going was close above Clovelly, so that a distance of some seven miles separated them. To walk this twice for the sake of lunching with a friend would seem to most young Americans too formidable a task to be at all worth while, but to our sturdy English pair it presented no difficulties. On they went, lightly and steadily, Imogen's elastic steps keeping pace easily with her brother's longer tread. There was a good deal of up and down hill to get over with, and whenever they topped a rise, green downs ending in wooded cliffs could be seen to the left, and beyond and below an expanse of white-flecked shimmering sea. A salt wind from the channel blew in their faces, full of coolness and refreshment, and there was no dust.

'I suppose we shall never see the ocean from where we are to live,' said Imogen, with a sigh.

'Well, hardly, considering it's about fifteen hundred miles away.'

'Fifteen hundred! Oh, Lion, you are surely exaggerating. Why, the whole of England is not so large as that, from Land's End to John O'Groat's House.'

'I should say not, nothing like it. Why Moggy, you've no idea how small our "right little, tight little island" really is. You could set it down plump in some of the States, New York, for instance, and there would be quite a tidy fringe of territory left all round it. Of course, morally, we are the standard of size for all the world, but geographically, phew!—Our size is little, though our hearts are great.'

'I think it's vulgar to be so big—not that I believe half you say, Lion. You've been over in America so long, and grown such a Yankee, that you swallow everything they choose to tell you. I've always heard about American brag——'

'My dear, there's no need to brag when the facts are there, staring you in the face. It's just a matter of feet and inches—anyone can do the measurement who has a tapeline. Wait till you see it. And as for its being vulgar to be big, why is the "right little, tight little" always stretching out her long arms to rope in new territory, in that case, I should like to know? It would be much eleganter to keep herself at home——'

'Oh, don't talk that sort of rot; I hate to hear you.'

'I must when you talk that kind of—well, let us say "rubbish". "Rot" is one of our choice terms which hasn't got over to the States yet. You're as opiniated and "narrer" as the little island itself. What do you know about America, anyway? Did you ever see an American in your life, child?'

'Yes, several. I saw Buffalo Bill last year, and lots of Indians and cowboys whom he had fetched over. And I saw Professor— Professor— what was his name? I forget, but he lectured on phrenology; and then there was Mrs. Geoff Templestowe.'

'Oh Mrs. Geoff—she's a different sort. Buffalo Bill and his show can hardly be treated as specimens of American society, and neither can your bump-man. But she's a fair sample of the nice kind; and you liked her, now didn't you? You know you did.'

'Well, yes, I did,' admitted Imogen, rather grudgingly. 'She was really quite nice, and good form, and all that, and Isabel said she was far and away the best sister-in-law yet, and the Squire took such a fancy to her that it was quite remarkable. But she cannot be used as an argument, for she's not the least like the American girls in the books. She must have had unusual advantages. And after all—nice as she was, she wasn't English. There was a difference somehow— you felt it though you couldn't say exactly what it was.'

'No, thank goodness—she isn't; that's just the beauty of it. Why should all the world be just alike? And what books do you mean, and what girls? There are all kinds on the other side, I can tell you. Wait till you get over to the High Valley and you'll see.'

This sort of discussion had become habitual of late between the brother and sister. Three years before, Lionel had gone out to Colorado, to 'look about and see how ranching suited him,' as he phrased it, and had decided that it suited him exactly. He had served a sort of apprenticeship to Geoffrey Templestowe, the son of an old Devonshire neighbour, who had settled in a place called High Valley, and, together with two partners, had built up a flourishing and lucrative cattle business, owning a large tract of grazing territory and great herds. One of the partners was now transferred to New Mexico, where the firm owned land also, and Mr. Young had advanced money to buy Lionel, who was now competent to begin for himself, a share in the business. He was now going out to remain permanently, and Imogen was going also, to keep his house and make a home for him till he should be ready to marry and settle down.

All over the world there are good English sisters doing this sort of thing. In Australia and New Zealand they are to be found, in Canada, and India, and the Transvaal — wherever English boys are sent to advance their fortunes.

Had her destination been Canada or Australia, Imogen would have found no difficulty in adjusting her ideas to it, but the United States were a terra incognita. Knowing absolutely nothing about them, she had constructed out of a fertile fancy and a few facts an altogether imaginary America, not at all like the real one; peopled by strange folk quite un-English in their ideas and ways, and very hard to understand and live with. In vain did Lionel protest and explain; his remonstrances were treated as proofs of the degeneracy and blindness induced by life in 'The States', and to all his appeals she opposed that calm, obstinate disbelief which is the weapon of a limited intellect and experience, and is harder to deal with than the most passionate convictions.

Unknown to herself a little sting of underlying jealousy tinctured these opinions. For many years Isabel Templestowe had been her favourite friend, the person she most admired and looked up to. They had been at school together—Isabel always taking the lead in everything, Imogen following and imitating. The Templestowes were better born than the Youngs, they took a higher place in the county; it was a distinction as well as a tender pleasure to be intimate in the house. Once or twice Isabel had gone to her married sister in London for a taste of the 'season'. No such chance had ever fallen to Imogen's lot, but it was next best to get letters, and hear from Isabel of all that she had seen and done; thus sharing the joys at second-hand, as it were.

Isabel had other intimates, some of whom were more to her than Imogen could be, but they lived at a distance and Imogen close at hand. Propinquity plays a large part in friendship as well as love. Imogen had no other intimate, but she knew too little of Isabel's other interests to be made uncomfortable about them, and was quite happy in her position as nearest and closest confidante until, four years before, Geoffrey Templestowe came home for a visit, bringing with him his American wife, whose name before her marriage had been Clover Carr, and whom some of you who read this will recognize as an old friend.

Young, sweet, pretty, very happy, and 'horribly well-dressed', as poor Imogen in her secret soul admitted, Clover easily and quickly won the liking of her 'people-in-law'. All the outlying sons and daughters who were within reach came home to make her acquaintance, and all were charmed with her. The Squire petted and made much of his new daughter and could not say enough in her praise. Mrs. Templestowe averred that she was as good as she was pretty, and as 'sensible' as if she had been born and brought up in England; and, worst of all, Isabel, for the time of their stay, was perfectly absorbed in Geoff and Clover, and though kind and affectionate when they met, had little or no time to spend on Imogen. She and Clover were of nearly the same age, each had a thousand interesting things to tell the other, both were devoted to Geoffrey — it was natural, inevitable, that they should draw together. Imogen confessed to herself that it was only right that they should do so, but it hurt all the same, and it was still a sore spot in her heart that Isabel should love Clover so much, and that they should write such long letters to each other. She was a conscientious girl, and she fought against the feeling and tried hard to forget it, but there it was all the same.

But while I have been explaining, the rapid feet of the two walkers had taken them past the Hoops Inn, and to the opening of a rough shady lane which made a short cut to the grounds of Stowe Manor, as the Templestowes place was called.

They entered by a private gate, opened by Imogen with a key which she carried, and found themselves on the slope of a hill overhung with magnificent old beeches. Farther down, the slope became steeper and narrowed to form the sharp 'chine' which cut the cliff seaward to the water's edge. The Manor-house stood on a natural plateau at the head of the ravine, whose steep green sides made a frame for the beautiful picture it commanded of Lundy Island, rising in bold outlines over seventeen miles of blue, tossing sea.

The brother and sister paused a moment to look for the hundredth time at this exquisite glimpse. Then they ran lightly down over the grass to where an interesting gravel-path led to the door. It stood hospitably open, affording a view of the entrance hall.

Such a beautiful old hall! Built in the time of the Tudors, with a great carven fireplace, mul-lioned windows in deep square bays, and a ceiling carved with fans, shields, and roses. 'Bow-pots' stood on the sills, full of rose-leaves and spices, huge antlers and trophies of weapons adorned the walls, and the polished floor, almost black with age, shone like a looking-glass.

Beyond opened a drawing-room, low-ceiled and equally quaint in build. The furniture seemed as old as the house. There was nothing with a modern air about it, except some Indian curiosities, a water-colour or two, the photographs of the family, and the fresh flowers in the vases. But the sun shone in, there was a great sense of peace and stillness, and beside a little wood-fire, which burned gently and did not hiss or crackle as it might have done elsewhere, sat a lovely old lady, whose fresh and peaceful and kindly face seemed the centre from which all the home look and comfort streamed. She was knitting a long silk stocking, a volume of Mudie's lay on her knee, and a Skye terrier, blue, fuzzy, and sleepy, had curled himself luxuriously in the folds of her dress.

This was Mrs. Templestowe, Geoff's mother and Clover's mother-in-law. She jumped up almost as lightly as a girl to welcome the visitors.

'Take your hat off, my dear,' she said to Imogen, 'or would you rather run up to Isabel's room? She was here just now, but her father called her off to consult about something in the hothouse. He won't keep her long—Ah, there she is now,' as a figure flashed by the window; 'I knew she would be here directly.'

Another second and Isabel hurried in, a tall, slender girl with thick, fair hair, blue eyes with dark lashes, and a look of breeding and distinction. Her dress, very simple in cut, suited her, and had that undefinable air of being just right which a good London tailor knows how to give. She wore no ornaments, but Imogen, who had felt rather well-dressed when she left home, suddenly hated her gown and hat, realized that her belt and ribbon did not agree, and wished for the dozenth time that she had the knack at getting the right thing which Isabel possessed.

'Her clothes grow prettier all the time, and mine get uglier,' she reflected. 'The Squire says she got points from Mrs. Geoff, and that the Americans know how to dress if they don't know anything else; but that's nonsense, of course—Isabel always did know how; she didn't need anyone to teach her.'

Pretty soon they were all seated at luncheon, a hearty and substantial meal, as befitted the needs of people who had just taken a seven-mile walk. A great round of cold beef stood at one end of the table, a chicken-pie at the other, and there were early peas and potatoes, a huge cherry-tart, a 'junket' equally large, strawberries, and various cakes and pastries, meant to be eaten with a smother of that delicacy peculiar to Devonshire, clotted cream. Everybody was very hungry, and not much was said till the first rage of appetite was satisfied.

'Ah!' said the Squire, as he filled his glass with amber-hued cider— 'you don't get anything so good as this to drink over in America, Lionel.'

'Indeed we do, sir. Wait till you taste our lemonade made with natural soda-water.'

'Lemonade? Phoo! Poor stuff I call it, cold and thin. I hope Geoff has some better tipple than that to cheer him in the High Valley.'

'Iced water,' suggested Lionel, mischievously.

'Don't talk to me about iced water. It's worse than lemonade. It's the perpetual use of ice which makes the Americans so nervous, I am convinced.'

'But, Papa, are they so nervous? Clover certainly isn't.'

'Ah! My little Clover—no, she wasn't nervous. She was nothing that she ought not to be. I call her as sweet a lass as any country need want to see. But Clover's no example; there aren't many like her, I fancy—eh, Lion?'

'Well, Squire, she's not the only one of the sort over there. Her sister, who married Mr. Page, our other partner, you know, is quite as pretty as she is, and as nice, too, though in a different way. And there's the oldest one—the wife of the naval officer, I'm not sure but you would like her the best of the three. She's a ripper in looks—tall, you know, with lots of go and energy, and yet as sweet and womanly as can be; you'd like her very much, you'd like all of them.'

'How is the unmarried one?—Joan, I think they call her,' asked Mrs. Templestowe.

'Oh!' said Lionel, rather confused, 'I don't know so much about her. She's only once been out to the valley since I was there. She seems a nice girl, and certainly she's mighty pretty.'

'Lion's blushing,' remarked Imogen. 'He always does blush when he speaks of that Miss Carr.'

'Rot!' muttered Lionel, with a wrathful look at his sister. 'I do nothing of the kind. But, Squire, when are you coming over to see for yourself how we look and behave? I think you and the Madam would enjoy a summer in the High Valley very much, and it would be no end of larks to have you. Isabel would like it of all things.'

'Oh, I know I should. I would start tomorrow, if I could. I'm coming across to make Clover and Imogen a long visit the first moment that Papa and Mamma can spare me.'

'That will be a long time to wait, I fear,' said her mother, sadly. 'Since Mr. Matthewson married and carried off poor Helen's children, the house has seemed so silent that except for you it would hardly be worthwhile to get up in the morning. We can't spare you at present, dear child.'

'I know, Mamma, and I shall never go till you can. The perfect thing would be that we should all go together.'

'Yes, if it were not for that dreadful voyage.'

'Oh, the voyage is nothing,' broke in the irrepressible Lionel. 'You just take some little pills; I forget the name of them, but they make you safe not to be sick, and then you're across before you know it. The ships are very comfortable—electric bells, welsh rabbits at bedtime, and all that, you know.'

'Fancy Mamma with a welsh rabbit at bedtime!—Mamma, who cannot even row down to Gallantry on the smoothest day without being upset! You must bait your hook with something else, Lionel, if you hope to catch her.'

'How would a trefoil of clover-leaves answer?' with a smile—'she, Geoff, and the boy.'

'Ah, that dear baby. I wish I could see the little fellow. He is so pretty in his picture,' sighed Mrs. Templestowe. 'That bait would land me if anything could, Lion. By the way, there are some little parcels for them, which I thought perhaps you would make room for, Imogen.'

'Yes, indeed, I'll carry anything with pleasure. Now I'm afraid we must be going. Mother wants me to step down to Clovelly with a message for the landlady of the New Inn, and I've set my heart upon walking once more to Gallantry Bower. Can't you come with us, Isabel? It would be so nice if you could, and it's my last chance.'

'Of course I will. I'll be ready in five minutes, if you really can't stay any longer.'

12

The three friends were soon on their way, under a low-hung sky, which looked near and threatening. The beautiful morning was fled.

'We had better cut down into the Hobby grounds and get under the trees, for I think it's going to be wet,' said Imogen.

The suggestion proved a wise one, for before they emerged from the shelter of the woods it was raining smartly, and the girls were glad of their waterproofs and umbrellas. Lionel, with hands in pockets, strode on, disdaining what he was pleased to call 'a little local shower'.

'You should see how it pours in Colorado,' he remarked. 'That's worth calling rain! Immense! Noah would feel perfectly at home in it!'

The tax of threepence each person, by which strangers are ingeniously made to contribute to the 'local charities', was not exacted of them at the New Road Gate, on the strength of their being residents, and personal friends of the owners of Clovelly Court. A few steps farther brought them to the top of a zig-zag path, sloping sharply downward at an angle of some sixty-five degrees, paved with broad stones, and flanked on either side by houses, no two of which occupied the same level, and which seemed to realize their precarious footing, and hug the rift in which they were planted as limpets hug a rock.

This was the so-called 'Clovelly Street', and surely a more extraordinary thing in the way of a street does not exist in the known world. The little village is built on the sides of a crack in a tremendous cliff; the 'street' is merely the bottom of the crack, into which the ingenuity of man has fitted a few stones, set slant-wise, with intersecting ridges on which the foot can catch as it goes slipping hopelessly down. Even to practised walkers the descent is difficult, especially when the stones are wet. The party from Stowe were familiar with the path, and had trodden it many times, but even they picked their steps and went 'delicately' like King Agag, holding up umbrellas in one hand, and with the other catching at garden palings and the edges of doorsteps to save themselves from pitching headlong, while beside them little boys and girls with the agility of long practice, went down merrily almost at a run, their heavy, flat-bottomed shoes making a clap-clap-clapping noise as they descended, like the strokes of a mallet on wood.

Looking up and above the quaint tenements that bordered the 'street', other houses equally quaint could be seen on either side rising above each other to the top of the cliff, in whose midst the crack which held the village is set. How it ever entered into the mind of man to utilize such a place for such a purpose it was hard to conceive. The eccentricity of level was endless, gardens topped roofs, gooseberry-bushes and plum-trees seemed growing out of chimneys, tall trees rose apparently from ridge-poles, and here and there against the sky appeared extraordinary wooden figures of colossal size, Mermaids and Britannias and Belle Savages, figureheads of forgotten ships which old sea-captains out of commission had set up in their gardens to remind them of perils past. The weather-beaten little houses looked centuries old, and all had such an air of having been washed accidentally into their places by a great tidal wave that the vines and flowers which overhung them affected the newcomer with a sense of surprise.

Down went the three, slipping and sliding, catching on and recovering themselves, till they came to a small, low-browed building dating back for a couple of centuries or so, which was the 'New Inn'. 'Old' and 'new' have a local meaning of their own in Clovelly which does not exactly apply anywhere else.

Up two little steps they passed into a narrow entry, with a parlour on one side and on the other a comfortable sort of housekeeper's room, where a fire was blazing in a grate with wide hobs. Both rooms as well as the entry were hung with plates, dishes, platters, and bowls, set thickly on the walls in groups of tens and scores and double-scores, as suited their shape and colour. The same ceramic decoration ran upstairs and pervaded the rooms above more or less; a more modem brick building on the opposite side of the street which was the 'annexe' of the Inn, was equally full;

hundreds and hundreds of plates and saucers and cups, English and Delft ware chiefly, and blue-and-white in colour. It had been the landlady's hobby for years past to form this collection of china, and it was now for sale to anyone who might care to buy.

Isabel and Lionel ran to and fro examining 'the great wall of China', as he termed it, while Imogen did her mother's errand to the landlady. Then they started again to mount the hill, which was an easier task than going down, passing on the way two or three parties of tourists holding on to each other, and shrieking and exclaiming; and being passed by a minute donkey with two sole-leather trunks slung on one side of him, and on the other a mountainous heap of handbags and valises. This is the only creature with four legs, bigger than a dog, that ever gets down the Clovelly street; and why he does not lose his balance, topple backward, and go rolling continuously down till he falls into the sea below, nobody can imagine. But the valiant little animal kept steadily on, assisted by his owner, who followed and assiduously whacked him with a stout stick, and he reached the top much sooner than any of his biped following. One cannot have too many legs in Clovelly—a centipede would find himself at an uncommon advantage.

At the top of the street is the 'Yellery Gate' through which our party passed into lovely park grounds topping a line of fine cliffs which lead to 'Gallantry Bower'. This is the name given to an enormous headland which falls into the sea with a sheer descent of nearly four hundred feet, and forms the western boundary of the Clovelly roadstead.

The path was charmingly laid out with belts of woodland and clumps of flowering shrubs. Here and there was a seat or a rustic summer-house, commanding views of the sea, now a deep intense blue, for the rain had ceased as suddenly as it came, and broad yellow rays were streaming over the wet grass and trees, whose green was dazzling in its freshness. Imogen drew in a long breath of the salt wind, and looked wistfully about her at the vivid turf, the delicate shimmer of blowing leaves, and the tossing ocean, as if trying to photograph each detail in her memory.

'I shall see nothing so beautiful over there,' she said. 'Dear old Devonshire, there's nothing like it.'

'Colorado is even better than "dear old Devonshire",' declared her brother; 'wait till you see Pike's Peak. Wait till I drive you through the North Cheyenne Canyon.'

But Imogen shook her head incredulously.

'Pike's Peak!' she answered, with an air of scorn. 'The name is enough; I never want to see it.'

'Well, you girls are good walkers, it must be confessed,' said Lionel, as they emerged on the crossing of the Bideford road where they must separate. 'Isabel looks as fresh as paint, and Moggy hasn't turned a hair. I don't think Mrs. Geoff could stand such a walk, or any of her family.'

'Oh, no, indeed; Clover would feel half-killed if she were asked to undertake a sixteen-mile walk. I remember, when she was here, we just went down to the pier at Clovelly for a row on the Bay and back through the Hobby, six miles in all, perhaps, and she was quite done up, poor dear, and had to go on to the sofa. I can't think why American girls are not better walkers—though there was that Miss Appleton we met at Zermatt, who went up the Matterhorn and didn't make much of it. Good-bye, Imogen; I shall come over before you start and fetch Mamma's parcels.'

CHAPTER TWO : MISS OPDYKE OF NEW YORK

The next week was a busy one. Packing had begun; and what with Mrs. Young's motherly desire to provide her children with every possible convenience for their new home, and Imogen's rooted conviction that nothing could be found in Colorado worth buying, and that it was essential to carry out all the tapes and sewing silk and buttons and shoe-thread and shoes and stationery and court-plaster and cotton cloth and and medicines that she and Lionel could possibly require during the next five years—it promised to be a long job.

In vain did Lionel remonstrate, and assure his sister that every one of these things could be had equally well at St. Helen's, where some of them went almost every day, and that extra baggage cost so much on the Pacific railways that the price of such commodities would be nearly doubled before she got them safely to the High Valley.

'Now what can be the use of taking two pounds of pins, for example?' he protested. Pins are as plenty as blackberries in America. And all those spools of thread too!'

'Reels of cotton, do you mean? I wish you would speak English, at least while we are in England. I shouldn't dare go without plenty of such things. American cotton isn't as good as ours; I've always been told that.'

'Well, it's good enough, as you'll find. And do make a place for something pretty; a few nice tea-cups for instance, and some things to hold flowers, and some curtain stuffs for the windows, and photographs. Geoff and Mrs. Geoff have made their house awfully nice, I can tell you. Americans think a deal of that sort of thing. All this haberdashery and hardware is ridiculous, and you'll be sorry enough that you didn't listen to me before you are through with it.'

'Mother has packed some cups already, I believe, and I'll take that white Minton jar if you like, but really I shouldn't think delicate things like that would be at all suitable in a new place like Colorado, where people must rough it as we are going to do. You are so infatuated about America,

Lion, that I can't trust your opinion at all.'

'I've been there, and you haven't,' was all that Lionel urged in answer. It seemed an incontrovertible argument, but Imogen made no attempt to overthrow it. She only packed on according to her own ideas, quite unconvinced.

It lacked only five days of their setting out when she and her brother walked into Bideford one afternoon for some last errands. It was June now, and the south of England was at its freshest and fairest. The meadows along the margin of the Torridge wore their richest green, the hill slopes above them were a bloom of soft colour. Each courtyard and garden shimmered with the gold of laburnums, or the purple and white of clustering clematis; and the scent of flowers came with every pufi of air.

As they passed up the side street, a carriage with three strange ladies in it drove by them. It stopped at the door of the New Inn—as quaint in build and even older than the New Inn of Clovelly. The ladies got out, and one of them, to Imogen's great surprise, came forward and extended her hand to Lionel.

'Mr. Young—it is Mr. Young, isn't it? You've quite forgotten me, I fear—Mrs. Page. We met at St. Helen's two years ago when I stopped to see my son. Let me introduce you to my daughter, the Comtesse de Conflans, and Miss Opdyke, of New York.'

Lionel could do no less than stop, shake hands, and present his sister, whereupon Mrs. Page urged them both to come in for a few minutes and have a cup of tea.

'We are here only till the evening train,' she explained, 'just to see Westward Ho and get a glimpse of the Amyas Leigh country. And I want to ask any quantity of questions about Clarence and his wife.

What! You are going out to the High Valley next week, and your sister too? Oh, that makes it absolutely impossible for me to let you off. You really must come in. There are so many messages I should like to send, and a cup of tea will be a nice rest for Miss Young after her long walk.'

'It isn't long at all,' protested Imogen; but Mrs. Page could not be gainsaid, and led the way upstairs to a sitting-room with a bay window overlooking the windings of the Torridge, which was crammed with quaint carved furniture of all sorts. There were buffets, cabinets, secretaries, delightful old claw-footed tables and sofas, and chairs whose backs and arms were a mass of griffins and heraldic emblems. Old oak was the speciality of the landlady of this New Inn, it seemed, as blue china was of the other. For years she had attended sales and poked about in farm-houses and attics, till little by little she had accumulated an astonishing collection. Many of the pieces were genuine antiques, but some had been constructed under her own eye from wood equally venerable—pew-ends and fragments of rood-screens purchased from a dismantled and ruined church. The effect was both picturesque and unusual.

Mrs. Page seated her guests in two wide, high-backed chairs, rang for tea, and began to question Lionel about affairs in the High Valley, while Imogen, still under the influence of surprise at finding herself calling on these strangers, glanced curiously at the younger ladies of the party. The Comtesse de Conflans was still young, and evidently had been very pretty, but she had a worn, dissatisfied air, and did not look happy. Imogen learned afterwards that her marriage, which was considered a triumph and a grand affair when it took place, had not turned out very well. Count Ernest de Conflans was rather a black sheep in some respects, had a strong taste for baccarat and rouge et noir, and spent so much of his bride's money at these amusements during the first year of their life together, that her friends became alarmed, and their interference had brought about a sort of amicable separation. Count Ernest lived in Washington, receiving a specified sum out of his wife's income, and she was travelling indefinitely in Europe with her mother. It was no wonder that she did not look satisfied and content.

'Miss Opdyke, of New York' was quite different and more attractive, Imogen thought. She had never seen anyone in the least like her. Rather tall, with a long slender throat, a waist of fabulous smallness, and hands which, in the gants de Suède, did not seem more than two inches wide, she gave the impression of being as fragile in make and as delicately fibred as an exotic flower. She had pretty, arch, grey eyes, a skin as white as a magnolia blossom, and a fluff of wonderful pale hair—artlessly looped and pinned to look as if it had blown by accident into its place—which yet exactly suited the face it framed. She was restlessly vivacious, her mobile mouth twitched with a hidden amusement every other moment; when she smiled she revealed pearly teeth and a dimple; and she smiled often. Her dress, apparently simple, was a wonder of fit and cut—a skirt of dark fawn-brown, a blouse of ivory-white silk, elaborately tucked and shirred, a cape of glossy brown fur whose high collar set off her pale vivid face, and a 'picture hat' with a wreath of plumes. Imogen, whose preconceived notion of an American girl included diamond ear-rings sported morning, noon, and night, observed with surprise that she wore no ornaments except one slender bangle. She had in her hand a great bunch of yellow roses, which exactly toned in with the ivory and brown of her dress, and she played with these and smelled them, as she sat on a high black-oak settle, and, consciously or unconsciously, made a picture of herself.

She seemed as much surprised and entertained at Imogen as Imogen could possibly be at her.

'I suppose you run up to London often,' was her first remark.

'N-o, not often.' In fact, Imogen had been in London only once in the whole course of her life.

'Dear me! Don't you? Why, how can you exist without it? I shouldn't think there would be anything to do here that was in the least amusing—not a thing. How do you spend your time?'

'I? I don't know, I'm sure. There's always plenty to do.'

'To do, yes; but in the way of amusement, I mean. Do you have many balls? Is there any gaiety going on? Where do you find your men?'

'No, we don't have balls often, but we have lawn parties, and tennis, and once a year there's a school feast.'

'Oh, yes, I know—children in gingham frocks and pinafores, eating buns and drinking milk-and-hot-water out of mugs. Rapturous fun it must be—but I think one might get tired of it in time. As for lawn parties I tried one in Fulham the other day, and I don't want to go to any more in England, thank you. They never introduced a soul to us, the band played out of tune, it was dull as ditch-water—just dreary, ill-dressed people wandering in and out, and trying to look as if five sour strawberries on a plate, and a thimbleful of ice-cream were bliss and high life and all the rest of it. The only thing really nice was the roses; those were delicious. Lady Mary Ponsonby gave me three —to make up for not presenting anyone to me, I suppose.'

'Do you still keep up the old fashion of introductions in America?' said Imogen with calm superiority. 'It's quite gone out with us. We take it for granted that wellbred people will talk to their neighbours at parties, and enjoy themselves well enough for the moment, and then they needn't be hampered with knowing them afterward. It saves a lot of complications not having to remember

names, or bow to people.'

'Yes, I know that's the theory, but I call it a custom introduced for the suppression of strangers. Of course, if you know all the people present, or who they are, it doesn't matter in the least; but if you don't, it makes it a ghastly mockery to try to enjoy yourself at a party. But do tell me some more about Bideford. I'm so curious about English country life. I've seen only London so far. Is it ever warm over here?'

'Warm?' vaguely, 'what do you mean?'

'I mean warm. Perhaps the word is not known over here, or doesn't mean the same thing. England seems to me just one degree better than Nova Zembla. The sun is a mere imitation sun. He looks yellow, like a real one, when you see him—which isn't often—but he doesn't burn a bit. I've had the shivers ever since we landed.' She pulled her fur cape closer about her ears as she spoke.

'Why, what can you want different from this?' asked Imogen, surprised. 'It's a lovely day. We haven't had a drop of rain since last night.'

'That is quite true, and remarkable as true; but somehow I don't feel any warmer than I did when it rained. Ah, here comes the tea. Let me pour it, Mrs. Page. I make awfully good tea. Such nice, thick cream! But, oh dear—here is more of that awful bread.'

It was a stout household loaf, of the sort invariable in south-country England, substantial, crusty, and tough, with a 'nubbin' on top, and in consistency something between pine wood and sole leather. Miss Opdyke, after filling her cups, proceeded to cut the loaf in slices, protesting as she did so that it 'creaked in the chewing', and that

'The muscular strength that it gave to her jaw Would last her the rest of her life.'

'Why, what sort of bread do you have in America?' demanded Imogen, astonished and offended by the frankness of these strictures. 'This is the sort everyone eats here. I'm sure it's excellent. What is there about it that you don't like?'

'Oh, everything. Wait till you taste our American bread, and you'll understand—or rather, our breads, for we have dozens of kinds, each more delicious than the last. Wait till you eat corn-bread and waffles.'

'I've always been told that the American food was dreadfully messy,' observed Imogen, nettled into reprisals; 'pepper on eggs, and all that sort of thing—very messy and nasty, indeed.'

'Well, we have deviated from the English method as to the eating of eggs, I admit. I know it's correct to chip the shell, and eat all the white at one end by itself, with a little salt, and then all the yellow in the middle, and last of all the white at the other end by itself; but there are bold spirits among us who venture to stir and mix. Fools rush in, you know; they will do it, even where Britons fear to tread.'

'We stopped at Northam to see Sir Amyas Leigh's house,' Mrs. Page was saying to Lionel. 'It's really very interesting to visit the spots where celebrated people have lived. There is a sad lack of such places in America. We are such a new country. Lilly and Miss Opdyke walked up to the hill where Mrs. Leigh stood to see the Spanish ship come in — quite fascinating, they said it was.'

'You must be sure to stay long enough in Boston to see the house where Silas Lapham. lived,' put in the wicked Miss Opdyke. 'One cannot see too much of places associated with famous people.'

'I don't remember any such name in American history,' said honest Imogen. ' "Silas Lap-ham," who was he?'

'A man in a novel, and Amyas Leigh is a man in another novel,' whispered Miss Opdyke. 'Mrs. Page isn't quite sure about him, but she doesn't like to confess as frankly as you do. She has forgotten, and fancies that he really lived in Queen Elizabeth's time; and the coachman was so solemnly sure that he did that it's not much wonder. I bought an old silver patch-box in a jeweller's shop on the High Street, and I'm going to tell my sister that it belonged to Ayacanora.'

'What an odd idea!'

'We are full of odd ideas in America, you know.'

'Tell me something about the States,' said Imogen. 'My brother is quite mad over Colorado, but he doesn't know much about the rest of it. I suppose the country about New York isn't very wild, is it?'

'Not very,' returned Miss Opdyke, with a twinkle. 'The buffalo are rarely seen now, and only two men were scalped by the Indians outside the walls of the city last year.'

'Fancy! And how do you pass your time? Is it a gay place?'

'Very. We pass our time doing all sorts of things. There's the Corn Dance and the Green Currant Dance and the Water Melon powwow, of course, and beside these, which date back to the early days of the colony, we have the more modern amusements, German opera and Italian opera and the theatre and subscription concerts. Then we have balls nearly every night in the season and dinner-parties and luncheons and lectures and musical parties, and we study a good deal and "slum" a little. Last winter I belonged to a Greek class and a fencing class, and a quartette club, and two private dancing classes, and a girls' working club, and an amateur theatrical society. We gave two private concerts for charities, you know, and acted the Antigone for the benefit of the Influenza Hospital. Oh, there is plenty to pass one's time in New York, I can assure you. And when other amusements fail, we can go outside the walls, with a guard of trappers, of course, and try our hand at converting the natives.'

'What tribe of Indians is it that you have near you?'

'The Tammanies—a very trying tribe, I assure you. It seems impossible to make any impression on them or teach them anything.'

'Fancy! Did you ever have any adventures yourself with the Indians? asked Imogen, deeply excited over this veracious resume of life in modem New York.

'Oh dear, yes—frequently.*

'Do tell me some of yours. This is so very interesting. Lionel never has said a word about the—Tallamies, did you call them?'

'Tammanies. Perhaps not; Colorado is so far off, you know. They have Piutes there—a different tribe entirely, and much less deleterious to civilization.'

'How sad! But about the adventures?'

'Oh, yes—well, I'll tell you of one; in fact it is the only exciting experience I ever had with the New York Indians. It was two years ago; I had just come out, and it was my birthday, and Papa said I might ride his new mustang, by way of a celebration. So we started, my brother and I, for a long country gallop. We were just on the other side of Central Park, barely out of the city, you see, when a sudden blood-curdling yell filled the air. We were horror-struck, for we knew at once what it must be—the war-cry of the savages. We turned of course and galloped for our lives, but the Indians were between us and the gates. We could see their terrible faces streaked with war-paint, and the tomahawks at their girdles, and we felt that all hope was over. I caught hold of Papa's lasso, which was looped round the saddle and cocked my revolving rifle—all the New York girls wear revolving rifles strapped round their waists,' continued Miss Opdyke, coolly, interrogating Imogen with her eyes as she spoke for signs of disbelief, but finding none, 'and I resolved to sell my life and scalp as dearly as possible. Just then, when all seemed lost, we heard a shout which sounded like music to our ears. A company of mounted Rangers were galloping out from the city. They had seen our peril from one of the watch-towers, and had hurried to our rescue.'

'How fortunate!' said Imogen, drawing a long breath. 'Well, go on— do go on.'

'There is little more to tell,' said Miss Opdyke, controlling with difficulty her inclination to laugh. 'The Head Ranger attacked the Tammany chief, whose name was Day Vidbehill—a queer name, isn't it?—and slew him after a bloody conflict. He gave me his brush, I mean his scalp-lock, afterwards, and it now adorns——' Here her amusement became ungovernable, and she went into fits of laughter, which Imogen's astonished look only served to increase.

'Oh!' she cried, between her paroxysms, 'you believed it all! It is too absurd, but you really believed it! I thought till just now that you were only pretending, to amuse me.'

'Wasn't it true, then?' said Imogen, her tardy wits waking slowly up to the conclusion.

'True! Why, my dear child, New York is the third city of the world in size—not quite so large as London, but approaching it. It is a great, brilliant, gay place, where everything under the sun can be bought and seen and done. Did you really think we had Indians and buffaloes close by us?'

'And haven't you?'

'Dear me, no. There never was a buffalo within a thousand miles of us, and not an Indian has come within shooting distance for half a century, unless he came by train to take part in a show. You mustn't be so easily taken in. People will impose upon you no end over in America, unless you are on your guard. What has your brother been about, not to explain things better?'

'Well, he has tried,' said Imogen, candidly, 'but I didn't half believe what he said, because it was so different from the things in the books. And then he is so in love with America that it seemed as if he must be exaggerating. He did say that the cities were just like our cities, only more so, and that though the West wasn't like England at all, it was very interesting to live in; but I didn't half listen to him, it sounded so impossible.'

'Live and learn. You'll have a great many surprises when you get across, but some of them will be pleasant ones, and I think you'll like it. Good-bye,' as Imogen rose to go; 'I hope we shall meet again sometime, and then you will tell me how you like Colorado, and the Piutes, and—waffles. I hope to live yet to see you stirring an egg in a glass with pepper and a "messy" lump of butter in true Western fashion. It's awfully good, I've always been told. Do forgive me for hoaxing you. I never thought you could believe me, and when I found that you did, it was irresistible to go on.'

'I can't make out at all about Americans,' said Imogen, plaintively, as after an effusive farewell from Mrs. Page and a languid bow from Madame de Conflans they were at last suffered to escape into the street. 'There seem to be so many different kinds. Mrs. Page and her daughter are not a bit like each other, and Miss Opdyke is quite different from either of them, and none of the three resembles Mrs. Geoffrey Templestowe in the least.'

'And neither does Buffalo Bill and your phrenological lecturer. Courage, Moggy. I told you America was a sizeable place. You'll begin to take in and understand the meaning of the variety show after you once get over there.'

'It was queer, but do you know I couldn't help rather liking that girl,' confessed Imogen later to Isabel Templestowe. 'She was odd, of course, and not a bit English, but you couldn't say she was bad form, and she was so remarkably quick and bright. It seemed as if she had seen all sorts of things and tried her hand on almost everything, and wasn't a bit afraid to say what she thought, or to praise and find fault. I told you what she said about English bread, and she was just as rude about our vegetables; she said they were only flavoured with hot water. What do you suppose she meant?'

'I believe they cook them quite differently in America. Geoff likes their way, and found a great deal of fault when he was at home with the cauliflower and the brussels sprouts. He declared that they had no taste, and that mint in green peas killed the flavour. Clover was too polite to say anything, but I could see that she thought the same. Mamma was quite put about with Geoff's new notions.'

'I must say that it seems rather impertinent and forth-putting for a new nation like that to be setting up opinions of its own, and finding fault with the good old English customs,' said Imogen, petulantly.

'Well, I don't know,' replied Isabel; 'we have made some changes ourselves. John of Gaunt or Harry Hotspur might find fault with us for the same reason, giving up the "good old customs" of rushes on the floor, for instance, and flagons of ale for breakfast. There were the stocks and the pillory too, and hanging for theft, and the torture of prisoners. Those were all in use more or less when the Pilgrims went to America, and I'm sure we're all glad that they were given up. The world must move, and I suppose it's but natural that the new nations should give it its impulse.'

'England is good enough for me,' replied the practical Imogen. 'I don't want to be instructed by new countries. It's like a child in a pinafore trying to teach its grandmother how to do things. Now, dear Isabel, let me hear about your mother's parcels.'

Mrs. Templestowe had wisely put her gifts into small compass. There were two dainty little frocks for her grandson, and a jacket of her own knitting, two pairs of knickerbocker stockings for Geoff, and for Clover a bit of old silver which had belonged to a Templestowe in the time of the Tudors—a double-handled porringer with a coat or arms engraved on its somewhat dented sides. Clover, like most Americans, had a passion for the antique; so this present was sure to please.

'And you are really off tomorrow,' said Isabel at the gate. 'How I wish I were going too.'

'And how I wish I were not going at all, but staying on with you,' responded Imogen. 'Mother says if Lionel isn't married by the end of three years she'll send Beatrice out to take my place. She'll be turned twenty then, and would like to come. Isabel, you'll be married before I get back, I know you will.'

'It's most improbable. Girls don't marry in England half so easily as in America. It will be you who will marry, and settle over there permanently.'

'Never!' cried Imogen.

Then the two friends exchanged a last kiss and parted.

'My love to Clover,' Isabel called back.

'Always Clover,' thought Imogen; but she smiled, and answered, 'Yes.'

CHAPTER THREE : THE LAST OF DEVON AND THE FIRST OF A MERICA

With the morrow came the parting from home. 'Farewell' is never an easy word to say when seas are to separate those who love each other, but the Young family uttered it bravely and resolutely. Lionel, who was impatient to get to work and to his beloved High Valley, was more than ready to go. His face, among the sober ones, looked aggressively cheerful.

'Cheer up, Mother,' he said, consolingly. 'You'll be coming over in a year or two with the Pater, and Moggy and I will give you such a good time as you never had in your lives. We'll all go up to Estes Park and camp out for a month. I can see you now coming down the trail on a burro—what fun it will be.'

'Who knows?' said Mrs. Young, with a smile that was half a sigh. She and her husband had sent a good many sons and daughters out into the world to seek their fortunes, and so far not one of them had come back. To be sure, all were doing well in their several ways— Cyril in India, where he had an excellent appointment, and the second boy in the army; two were in the navy, and Tom and Giles in Van Diemen's Land, where they were making a very good thing out of a sheep ranch. There was no reason why Lionel should not be equally lucky with his cattle in Colorado; there were younger children to be considered; it was 'all in the day's work', the natural thing. Large families must separate, parents could not expect to keep their grown boys and girls with them always. So they dismissed the two who were now going forth cheerfully, uncomplainingly, and with their blessing, but all the same it was not pleasant; and Mrs. Young shed some quiet tears in the privacy of her own room, and her husband looked very serious as he strode down the Southampton docks after saying good-bye to his children on board the steamer.

Imogen had never been on a great sea-going vessel before, and it struck her as being very crowded and confused as well as bewilderingly big. She stood clutching her bags and bundles nervously and feeling homesick and astray while farewells and greetings went on about her, and the people who were going and those who were to stay behind seemed mixed in an inextricable tangle on the decks. Then a bell rang, and gradually the groups separated; those who were not going formed themselves into a black mass on the pier; there was a great fluttering of handkerchiefs, a plunge of the screw, and the steamer was off.

Lionel, who had been seeing to the baggage, now appeared, and took Imgoen down to her stateroom, advising her to get out all her warm things and make ready for a rough night.

'There's quite a sea on outside,' he remarked. 'We're in for a rolling if not for a pitching.'

'Lion!' cried Imogen, indignantly. 'Do you mean to say that you suppose I'm going to be sick—I, a Devonshire girl born and bred, who have lived by the sea all my life? Never!'

'Time will show,' was the oracular response. 'Get the rugs out, anyway, and your brushes and combs and things, and advise Miss What-d'-you-call-her to do the same.'

'Miss What-d'-you-call-her' was Imogen's room-mate, a perfectly unknown girl, who had been to her imagination one of the chief bugbears of the voyage. She was curled up on the sofa in a tumbled little heap when they entered the stateroom, had evidently been crying, and did not look at all formidable, being no older than Imogen, very small and shy, a soft, dark-eyed appealing creature, half English, half Belgic by extraction, and going out, it appeared, to join a lover who for three years had been in California making ready for her. He was to meet her in New York, with a clergyman in his pocket, so to speak, and as soon as the marriage ceremony was performed, they were to set out for their ranch in the San Gabriel Valley, to raise grapes, dry raisins, and 'live happily all the days of their lives afterward', like the prince and princess of a fairy tale.

These confidences were not made immediately or all at once, but gradually, as the two girls became acquainted, and mutual suffering endeared them to each other. For, spite of Imogen's Devonshire bringing up, the English Channel proved too much for her, and she had to endure two pretty bad days before, promoted from gruel to dry toast, and from dry toast to beef-tea, she was able to be helped on deck, and seated, well wrapped up, in a reclining chair to inhale the cold, salty wind which was the best and only medicine for her particular kind of ailment. The chair next hers was occupied by a pretty, dark-eyed, and very lady-like woman with whom Lionel had apparently made an acquaintance; for he said, as he tucked Imogen's rugs about her, 'Here's my sister at last, you see;' which off-hand introduction the lady acknowledged with a pleasant smile, saying she was glad to see Miss Young able to be up. Her manner was so unaffected and cordial that Imogen's stiffness melted under its influence, and before she knew it they were talking quite like old acquaintances.

Imogen was struck by the sweet voice of the stranger, with its well-bred modulations, and also by the good taste and perfection of all her little appointments, from the down pillow at top of her chair to the fur-trimmed shoes on a pair of particularly pretty feet at the other end. She set her down in her own mind as a London dame of fashion—perhaps a countess, or a Lady Something-or-other, who was going out to see America.

'Your brother tells me this is your first voyage,' said the lady.

'Yes. He has been out before, but none of us were with him. It is all perfectly strange to me' —with a sigh.

'Why do you sigh? Don't you expect to like it?'

'Why no, not like it exactly. Of course I'm glad to be with Lionel and of use to him, but I didn't come away from home for pleasure.'

'Pleasure must come to you, then,' said the lady, with a smile. 'And really I don't see why it shouldn't. In the first place you are acting the part of a good sister; and you know the adage about duty performed making rainbows in the soul. And then Colorado is a beautiful State, with the finest of mountain views, a wonderful climate, and such wild flowers as grow nowhere else. I have some friends living there who are quite infatuated about it. They say there is no place so delightful in the world.'

'That is just the way with my brother. It's really absurd the way he talks about it. You would think it was better than England!'

'It is sure to be very different; but all the same, you will like it, I think.'

'I hope so' — doubtfully.

Just then came an interruption in the shape of a tall girl of fifteen or sixteen, with a sweet, childish face, who came running down the deck accompanied by a maid, and seized the strange lady's hand.

'Mamma,' she began, 'the first officer says that if you are willing he will take me across to the bows to see the rainbows on the foam. May I go? He says Anne can go too.'

'Yes, certainly, if Mr. Graves will take charge of you. But first speak to this young lady, who is the sister of Mr. Young, who was so kind about playing ship-coil with you yesterday, and tell her you are glad she is able to be on deck. Then you can go, Amy.'

Amy turned a pair of beautiful, long-lashed, grey eyes on Imogen.

'I'm glad you're better, Miss Young. Mamma and I were sorry you were so sick,' she said, with a frank politeness that was charming. 'It must be very disagreeable.'

'Haven't you been sick, then?' said Imogen, holding fast the little hand that was put into hers.

'No, I'm never sick now. I was, though, the first time we came over, and I behaved awfully. Do you recollect, Mamma?'

'Only too well,' said her mother, laughing. 'You were like a caged bird, beating yourself against the bars in desperation.'

Amy lingered a moment, while a dimple played in her pink cheek as if she were moved by some amusing remembrance.

'Ah, there's Mr. Graves,' she said. 'I must go. I'll come back presently and tell you about the rainbows. Mamma.'

'I suppose most of these people on board are Americans,' said Imogen after a little pause. 'It's always easy to tell them, don't you think?'

'Not always. Yes, I suppose a good many of them are—or call themselves so.'

'What do you mean by "call themselves so"? That girl is one, I am sure,' indicating a pretty, stylish young person, who was talking rather too loudly for good taste with the ship's doctor.

'Yes, I imagine she is.'

'And those people over there,' pointing to a large red-bearded man who lay back in a sea-chair reading a novel, by the side of a fat wife who read another, while their little boy raced up and down the deck quite unheeded, and amused himself by pulling the rugs off the knees of the sicker passengers. 'They are Americans, I know! Did you ever see such creatures? The idea of letting that child make a nuisance of himself like that! No one but an American would allow it. I've always heard that children in the States do exactly as they please, and the grown people never interfere with them in the least.'

'General rules are dangerous things,' said her neighbour, with an odd little smile. 'Now, as it happens, I know all about those people. They call themselves Americans because they have lived in Buffalo for ten years and are naturalized; but he was born in Scotland and she in Wales, and the child doesn't belong exactly to any country, for he happened to be born at sea. You see you can't always tell.'

'Do you mean, then, that they are English, after all?' cried Imogen, disconcerted and surprised.

'Oh, no. Everybody is an American who has taken the oath of allegiance. Those Polish Jews over there are Americans, and that Italian couple also, and the big party of Germans who are sitting between the boats. The Germans have a large shop in New York, and go out every year to buy

goods and tell their relations how superior the United States are to Breslau. They are all Americans, though you would scarcely suppose it to look at them. America is like a pudding—plums from one part of the world, and spice from another, and flour and sugar and flavouring from somewhere else, but all known by the name of pudding.'

'How very, very odd. Somehow I never thought of it before in that light. Are there no real Americans, then? Are they all foreigners who have been naturalized?'

'Oh, no. It is not so bad as that. There are a great many "real Americans". I am one, for example.'

'You!' There was such a world of unfeigned surprise in Imogen's tone that it was impossible for her new friend not to laugh.

'I. Did you not know it? What did you take me for?'

'Why, English of course, like myself. You are exactly like an English person.'

'I suppose you mean it for a compliment; thank you, therefore. I like England very much, so I don't mind being taken for an English woman.'

'Of course you don't,' said Imogen, staring. 'It's the height of an American's ambition, I've always heard, to be thought English.'

'There you are mistaken. There are a few foolish people who feel so, no doubt, and all of us would be glad to copy what is best and nicest in English ways and manners, but a really good American likes his own country best of all, and would rather seem to belong to it than any other.'

'And I was thinking how different your daughter is from the American girls!' said Imogen, continuing her own train of thought; 'and how her manners were so pretty, and did such credit to w, and would surprise people over there! How very odd. I shall never get to understand the Americans. They're so different from each other as well as from us. There were some ladies from New York at

Bideford the other day—a Mrs. Page and a Comtesse de Something-or-other, her daughter, and a Miss Opdyke from New York. She was very pretty and really quite nice, though rather queer, but all three were as unlike each other as they could be. Do you know them in America?'

'Not Miss Opdyke; but I have met Mrs. Page once in Europe a good while since. It was before her daughter was married. She is a relative of my sister-in-law, Mrs. Worthington.'

'Do you mean the Mrs. Worthington whose husband is in the navy? Why, that's Mrs. Geoffrey Templestowe's sister!'

'Do you know Clover Templestowe, then?' said the lady, surprised in her turn. 'That is really curious. Was it in England that you met?'

'Yes, and we are on our way to her neighbourhood now. My brother has bought a share in Geoff's business, and we are going to live near them at High Valley.'

'I do call this an extraordinary coincidence. Amy, come here and listen. This young lady is on her way to Colorado, to live close to Aunt Clover; what do you think of that for a surprise?

I don't wonder that you open your eyes so wide. Isn't it just like a story-book that she should have come and sat down in the next chair to ours?'

'It's so funny that I can't believe it, till I take time to think,' said Amy, perching herself on the arm of her mother's seat. 'Just think, you'll see Elsie and her baby, and Aunt Clover's baby, and Uncle Geoff and Phil, and all of them. It's the beautifulest place out there that you ever saw. There are

whole droves of horses, and you ride all the while, and when you're not riding you can pick flowers and play with the babies. Oh, I wish I were going with you; it would be such fun!'

'But aren't you coming?' said Imogen, much taken by the frankness of the little American maid. 'Coax Mamma to fetch you out this summer, and come and make me a visit, We're going to have a little cabin of our own, and I'd be delighted to have you. Is it far from where you live?'

'Well, it's what you would call "a goodish bit" in England,' replied Mrs. Ashe, 'two thousand miles or so, nearly three days' journey. Amy would be charmed to come, I am sure, but I am afraid the distance will stand in her way. One doesn't "step out" to Colorado every summer, but perhaps we may be there some day, and then we shall certainly hope to see you.'

This encounter with Mrs. Ashe, who was, in a way, part of the family with whom Imogen expected to be most intimately associated in America, made the remainder of the voyage very pleasant. They sat together for hours every day, talking, and reading, and gradually Imogen waked up to the fact that American life and society was a much more complex and less easily understood affair than she had imagined.

The weather was favourable when the first rough days were past, and after they rounded the curve of the wide sea hemisphere and began to near the American coast it became beautiful, with high-arching skies and very bright sunsets. Accustomed to the low-hung greys and struggling sunbeams of southern England, Imogen could not get used to these novelties. Her surprise over the dazzle of the day and the clear, vivid blue of the heavens was a continual amusement and joy to Mrs. Ashe, who took a patriotic pride in her own climate, and, as it were, made herself responsible for it.

Then came the eventful morning, when, rousing to the first glow of dawn, they found the screw motionless, and the steamer lying off a green island, with a big barrack-building on it, over which waved the American flag. The health officer made his visit, and before long they were steaming up the wide bay of New York, between green, flowery shores, under the colossal Liberty, whose outstretched arm seemed to point to the dim rich mass of roofs and towers and spires of the city which lay beyond. Then they neared the landing-stage, where a black mass of people stood waiting for them, and Amy gave a cry of delight as she saw a gold-banded cap among them, and recognized her Uncle Ned.

The little Anglo-Belgian had been more or less ill all the way over, and looked pale and wan, though still very pretty, as she stood with the rest, gazing at the crowd of faces, all of whose eyes were turned toward the steamer.

Imogen, who had helped her to dress, remained protectingly by her side.

'What shall you do if he doesn't happen to be there?' she asked, smitten with a sudden fear. 'Something might detain him, you know.'

'I—I—am not sure,' turning pale. 'Oh, yes, I am,' rallying. 'He have aunt in Howbokken. I go there and wait. But he not fail; he will be here.' Then her eyes suddenly lit up, and she exclaimed with a little shriek of joy, 'He are here! That is he standing by the big timber. My Karl! My Karl! He are here!'

There indeed he was, foremost in the throng, a tall, brown, handsome fellow, with a nice, strong face, and such a look of love and expectation in his eyes that prosaic Imogen suddenly felt that it might be worth while, after all, to cross half the world to meet a look and a husband like that—a fact which she had disbelieved till now, demurring also in her private mind as to the propriety of such a thing. It was pretty to see the tender happiness in the girl's face, and the answering expression of her lover's. It seemed to put poetry and pathos into an otherwise commonplace scene.

The gangplank was lowered, a crowd of people surged ashore, to be met by a corresponding surge from the onlookers, and in the midst of it Lieutenant Worthington leaped aboard and hastened to where his sister stood waiting for him.

'You're coming up to Newport with me at five-thirty,' were his first words. 'Katy's all ready, and means to sit up till the boat gets in at two-thirty, keeping a little supper hot and hot for you. The Torpedo Station is in its glory just now, and there's going to be a great explosion on Thursday, which Amy will enjoy.'

'How lovely!' cried Amy, clinging to her uncle's arm. 'I love explosions. Why didn't Tanta come too? I'm in such a hurry to see her.'

Then Mr. Worthington asked to be introduced to Imogen and Lionel, and explained that acting on a request from Geoffrey Templestowe, he had taken rooms for them at a hotel and secured their tickets and sleeping sections in the 'Limited' train for the next day.

'And I told them to save two seats for Rip Van Winkle tonight till you got there,' he added. 'If you're not too tired I advise you to go. Jefferson is an experience which you ought not to miss, and you may never have another chance.'

'How awfully kind your brother is,' said the surprised Imogen to Mrs. Ashe; 'all this trouble and he never saw either of us before! It's very good of him.'

'Oh, that's nothing. That's the way American men do. They are perfect dears, there's no doubt as to that, and they don't consider anything a trouble which helps along a friend or a friend's friend. It's a matter of course over here.'

'Well, I don't consider it a matter of course at all. I think it extraordinary, and it was so very nice of Geoff to send word to Lion.'

Then they parted. Meanwhile the little roommate had been having a private conference with her 'young man'. She now joined Imogen.

'Karl says we shall be married directly, in a church in half an hour,' she told her. 'And oh, won't you and Mr. Young come to be with us? It is so sad not to have one friend when one is married.'

It was impossible to refuse this request; so it happened that the very first thing Imogen did in America was to attend a wedding. It took place in an old church, pretty far down town; and she always afterward carried in her mind the picture of it, dim and sombre in colouring, with the afternoon sun pouring in through a rich rose window and throwing blue and red reflections on the little group of five at the altar, while from outside came the din of wheels and the unceasing tread of busy feet. The service was soon over, the signatures were made, and the little bride went down the chancel on her husband's arm, with her face appropriately turned to the west, and with such a look of secure and unfearing happiness upon it as was good to see. It was an unusual and typical scene with which to begin life in a new country, and Imogen liked to think afterward that she had been there.

Then followed a long drive up town over rough ill-laid pavements, through dirty streets, varied by dirtier streets, and farther up, by those that were less dirty. Imogen had never seen anything so shabby as the poorest of the buildings that they passed, and certainly never anything quite so fine as the best of them. Squalor and splendour jostled each other side by side; everywhere there was the same endless throng of hurrying people, and everywhere the same abundance of flowers for sale, in pots, in baskets, in bunches, making the whole air of the streets sweet. Then they came to the hotel, and were shown to their rooms—high up, airy, and nicely furnished, though Imogen was at first disposed to cavil at the absence of bed-curtains.

'It looks so bare,' she complained. 'At home such a thing would be considered very odd, very odd indeed. Fancy a bed without curtains!'

'After you've spent one hot night in America you'll be glad enough to fancy it,' replied her brother. 'Stuffy old things. It's only in cold weather that one could endure them over here.'

The first few hours on shore after a voyage have a delightfulness all their own. It is so pleasant to bathe and dress without having to hold on and guard against lurches and tips. Imogen went about her toilet well-pleased; and her pleasure was presently increased when she found on her dressing-table a beautiful bunch of summer roses, with 'Mrs. Geoffrey Temple-stowe's love and welcome' on a card lying beside it. Thoughtful Clover had written to Ned Worthington to see to this little attention, and the pleasure it gave went even farther than she had hoped.

'I declare,' said Imogen, sitting down with the flowers before her, 'I never knew anybody so kind as they all are. I don't feel half so homesick as I expected. I must write Mamma about these roses. Of course Mrs. Geoff does it for Isabel's sake; but all the same it is awfully nice of her, and I shall try not to forget it.'

Then, when, after finishing her dressing, she drew the blinds up and looked from the windows, she gave a cry of sheer pleasure, for there beneath was spread out a beautiful wide distance of park with feathery trees and belts of shrubs, behind which the sun was making ready to set in a crimson sky. There was a balcony outside the windows, and Imogen pulled a chair out on it to enjoy the view.

Carriages were rolling in at the Park gates, looking exactly like the equipages one sees in London, with fat coachmen, glossy horses, and jingling silvered harness. Girls and young men were cantering along the bridle-paths, and throngs of well-dressed people filled the walks. Beyond was a fairy lake, where gondolas shot to and fro; a band was playing; from still farther away came a peal of chimes from a church tower.

'And this is New York!' thought Imogen. Then her thoughts reverted to Miss Opdyke and her tale of the Tammany Indians, and she flushed with sudden vexation.

'What an idiot she must have considered me!' she reflected.But her insular prejudices revived in full force as a knock was heard, and a coloured boy, entering with a tinkling pitcher, inquired, 'Did you ring for ice-water, lady?'

'No!' said Imogen sharply; 'I never drink iced water. I rang for hot water, but I got it more than an hour ago.'

'Beg pardon, lady.'

'Why on earth does he call me "lady"?' she murmured. 'So tiresome and vulgar!'

Then Lionel came for her, and they went down to dinner—a wonderful repast, with soups and fishes and vegetables quite unknown to her; a bewildering succession of meats and entrees, strawberries such as she had supposed did not grow outside of England, raspberries and currants such as England never knew, and wonderful blackberries, of great size and sweetness, bursting with purple juice. There were ices too, served in the shapes of apples, pears, and stalks of asparagus, which dazzled her country eyes not a little, while the whole was a terror and astonishment to her thrifty English mind.

'Lionel, don't keep on ordering things so,' she protested. 'We are eating our heads off as it is, I am sure.'

'My dear young friend, you are come to the Land of Fat Things,' he replied. 'Dinner costs just the same, once you sit down to it, whether you have a biscuit and a glass of water, or all these things.'

'I call it a sinful waste, then,' she retorted. 'But all the same, since it is so, I'll take another ice.'

' "First endure, then pity, then embrace," ' quoted her brother. 'That's right, Moggy; pitch in, spoil the Egyptians. It doesn't hurt them, and it will do you lots of good.'

From the dinner-table they went straight to the theatre, having decided to follow Lieutenant Worthington's advice and see Rip Van Winkle. And then they straightway fell under the spell of a magician who has enchanted many thousands before them, and for the space of two hours forgot themselves, their hopes and fears and expectations, while they followed the fortunes of the idle, lovable, unpractical Rip, up the mountain to his sleep of years, and down again, white-haired and tottering, to find himself forgotten by his kin and a stranger in his own home. People about them were weeping on relays of pocket-handkerchiefs, hanging them up one by one as they became soaked, and beginning on others. Imogen had but one handkerchief, but she cried with that till she had to borrow Lionel's; and he, though he professed to be very stoical, could not quite command his voice as he tried to chaff her in a whisper on her emotions, and begged her to 'dry up' and remember that it was only a play after all, and that presently Jefferson would discard his white hair and wrinkles, go home to a good supper, and make a jolly end to the evening.

It was almost too exciting for a first night on shore, and if Imogen had not been so tired, and if her uncurtained bed had not proved so deliciously comfortable, she would scarcely have slept as she did till half-past seven the next morning, so that they had to scramble through breakfast not to lose their train. Once started in the

'Limited', with a library and a lady's maid, a bath and a bed at her disposal, and just beyond a daintily appointed dinner-table adorned with fresh flowers—all at forty miles an hour—she had leisure to review her situation and be astonished. Bustling cities shot past them—or seemed to shoot—beautifully kept country-seats, shabby suburbs where goats and pigs mounted guard over shanties and cabbage beds, great tracts of wild forest, factory towns black with smoke, rivers winding between blue hill ridges, prairie-like expanses so overgrown with wild flowers that they looked all pink or all blue—everything by turns and nothing long. It seemed the sequence of the unexpected, a succession of rapidly changing surprises, for which it was impossible to prepare beforehand.

'I shall never learn to understand it,' thought poor perplexed Imogen.

CHAPTER FOUR : IN THE HIGH VALLEY

Meanwhile, as the 'Limited' bore the young English travellers on their western way, a good deal of preparation was going on for their benefit in that special nook of the Rocky Mountains toward which their course was directed. It was one of those clear-cut, jewel-like mornings which seemed peculiar to Colorado, with dazzling gold sunshine, a cloudless sky of deep sapphire blue, and air which had touched the mountain snows somewhere in its nightly blowing, and still carried on its wings the cool pure zest of the contact.

Hours were generally early in the High Valley, but today they were a little earlier than usual, for everyone had a sense of much to be done. Clover Templestowe did not always get up to administer to her husband and brother-in-law their 'stirrup-cup' of coffee; but this morning she was prompt at her post, and after watching them ride up the valley, and standing for a moment at the open door for a breath of the scented wind, she seated herself at her sewing-machine. A steady whirring hum presently filled the room, rising to the floor above and quickening the movements there. Elsie, running rapidly downstairs half an hour later, found her sister with quite a pile of little cheesecloth squares and oblongs folded on the table near her.

'Dear me! Are those the Youngs' curtains you are doing?' she asked. 'I fully meant to get down early and finish my half. That wretched little Phillida elected to wake up and demand " 'tories" from one o'clock till a quarter past two.

"Hence these tears." I overslept myself without knowing it.'

Phillida was Elsie's little girl, two years and a half old now, and Dr. Carr's namesake.

'How bad of her!' said Clover, smiling. 'I wish children could be born with a sense of the fitness of times and seasons. Geoffy is pretty good as to sleeping, but he is dreadful about eating. Half the time he doesn't want anything at dinner; and then at half past three, or a quarter to eight, or ten minutes after twelve, or some such uncanonical hour, he is so ragingly hungry that he can scarcely wait till I fetch him something. He is so tiresome about his bath too. Fancy a young semi-Briton objecting to "tub". I've circumvented him today, however, for Geoff has promised to wash him while you and I go up to set the new house in order. Baby is always good with Geoff.'

'So he is,' remarked Elsie as she moved about giving little tidying touches here and there to books and furniture. 'I never knew a father and child who suited each other so perfectly. Phil flirts with Clarence and he is very proud of her notice, but I think they are mutually rather shy; and he always touches her as though she were a bit of eggshell china, that he was afraid of breaking.'

The room in which the sisters were talking bore little resemblance to the bare ranch-parlour of old days. It had been enlarged by a semicircular bay window towards the mountain view, which made it half as long again as it then was; and its ceiling had been raised two feet on the occasion of Clarence's marriage, when great improvements had been undertaken to fit the 'hut' for the occupation of two families. The solid redwood beams which supported the floor above had been left bare, and lightly oiled to bring out the pale russet-orange colour of the wood. The spaces between the beams were rough-plastered; and on the decoration of this plaster, while in a soft state, a good deal of time had been expended by Geoffrey Templestowe, who had developed a turn for household art, and seemed to enjoy lying for hours on his back on a staging, clad in pyjamas and indenting the plaster with rosettes and sunken half-rounds, using a croquet ball and a butter stamp alternately, the whole being subsequently finished by a coat of dull gold paint. He and Clover had themselves hung the walls with its pale orange-brown paper; a herder with a turn for carpentry had laid the new floor of narrow redwood boards. Clover had stained the striped pattern along its edges. In that remote spot, where trained and regular assistance could be had only at great trouble and expense, it was desirable that everyone should utilize whatever faculty or accomplishment he or she possessed, and the result was certainly good. The big, homelike room, with its well-chosen colours and look of taste and individuality, left nothing to be desired in the way of comfort, and was far prettier and more original than if ordered cut-and-dried from some artist in effects, to whom its doing would have been simply a job and not an enjoyment.

Clover's wedding presents had furnished part of the rugs and etchings and bits of china which ornamented the room, but Elsie's, who had married into a 'present-giving connection', as her sister Johnnie called it, did even more. Each sister was supposed to own a private sitting-room, made out of the little sleeping-chambers of what Clarence Page stigmatized as the 'beggarly bachelor days', which were thrown together two in one on either side the common room. Clover and Elsie had taken pains and pleasure in making these pretty and different from each other, but as a matter of fact the 'private' parlours were not private at all; for the two families were such very good friends that they generally preferred to be together. And the rooms were chiefly of use when the house was full of guests, as in the summer it sometimes was, when Johnnie had a girl or two staying with her, or a young man with a tendency toward corners, or when Dr. Carr wanted to escape from his young people and analyse flowers at leisure or read his newspaper in peace and quiet.

The big room in the middle was used by both families as a dining and sitting place. Behind it another had been added, which served as a sort of mixed library, office, dispensary, and storage-room, and over the four, extending to the very edge of the wide verandas which flanked the house on three sides, were six large bedrooms. Of these each family owned three, and they had an equal right as well to the spare rooms in the building which had once been the kitchen. One of these, called 'Phil's room', was kept as a matter of course for the use of that young gentleman, who, while nominally studying law in an office at St. Helen's, contrived to get out to the Valley very frequently. The interests of the party were so identical that the matter of ownership seldom came up, and signified little. The sisters divided the housekeeping between them amicably, one supplementing the other; the improvements were paid for out of a common purse; their guests, being equally near and dear, belonged equally to all. It was an ideal arrangement, which one quick tongue or jealous or hasty temper would have brought to speedy conclusion, but which had now lasted to the satisfaction of all parties concerned for nearly four years.

That Clarence and Elsie should fancy each other had been a secret though unconfessed dream of Clover's ever since her own engagement, when Clarence had endeared himself by his manly behaviour and real unselfishness under trying circumstances. But these dreams are rarely gratified, and she was not at all prepared to have hers come true with such unexpected ease and rapidity. It happened on this wise. Six months after her marriage, when she and Geoff and Clarence, working together, had just got the 'hut' into a state to receive visitors, Mr. and Mrs. Dayton, who had never forgotten or lost their interest in their pretty fellow-traveller of two years before, hearing from Mrs. Ashe how desirous Clover was of a visit from her father and sisters, wrote and asked the Carrs to go out with them in car 47 as far as Denver, and be picked up and brought back two months later when the Daytons returned from Alaska. The girls were wild to go, it seemed an opportunity too good to be lost; so the invitation was accepted, and, as sometimes happens, the kindness shown had an unlooked-for return.

Mr. Dayton was seized with a sudden ill turn on the journey, of a sort to which he was subject, and Dr. Carr was able not only to help him at the moment, but to suggest a regimen and treatment which was of permanent benefit to him. Doctor and patient grew very fond of each other, and every year since, when car 47 started on its western course, urgent invitations came for any or all of them to take advantage of it and go out to see Clover; whereby that hospitable housekeeper gained many visits which otherwise she would never have had, Colorado journeys being expensive luxuries.

But this is anticipating. No visit, they all agreed, ever compared with that first one, when they were so charmed to meet, and everything was new and surprising and delightful. The girls were enchanted with the Valley, the climate, the wild fresh life, the riding, the flowers, with Clover's little home made pretty and convenient by such simple means, while Dr. Carr revelled in the splendid air, which seemed to lift the burden of years from his shoulders.

And presently began the excitement of watching Clarence Page's rapid and successful wooing of Elsie. No grass grew under his feet this time, you may be sure. He fell in love the very first evening, deeply and heartily, and he lost no opportunity of letting Elsie know his sentiments. There was no rival in his way at the High Valley or elsewhere, and the result seemed to follow as a matter of course. They were engaged when the party went back to Burnet, and married the following spring, Mr. Dayton fitting up 47 with all manner of sentimental and delightful appointments, and sending the bride and bridegroom out in it—as a wedding present, he said, but in truth the car was a repository of wedding presents, for all the rugs and portieres and silken curtains and brass plaques and pretty pottery with which it was adorned, and the flower-stands and Japanese kakemonos, were to disembark at St. Helen's and help to decorate Elsie's new home. All went as was planned, and Clarence's life from that day to this had been, as Clover mischievously told him, one paean of thanksgiving to her for refusing him and opening the way to real happiness. Elsie suited him to perfection.

Everything she said and did and suggested was exactly to his mind, and as for looks, Clover was dear and nice as could be, of course, and pretty—well, yes, people would undoubtedly consider her a pretty little woman; but as for any comparison between the two sisters, it was quite out of the question! Elsie had so decidedly the advantage in every point, including that most important point of all, that she preferred him to Geoff Templestowe and loved him as heartily as he loved her. Happiness and satisfied affection had a wonderfully softening influence on Clarence, but it was equally droll and delightful to Clover to see how absolutely Elsie ruled, how the least indication of her least finger availed to mould Clarence to her will— Clarence, who had never yielded easily to anyone else in the whole course of his life!

So the double life flowed smoothly on in the High Valley, but not quite so happily at Burnet, where Dr. Carr, bereft of four out of his six children, was left to the companionship of the steady Dorry, and what he was pleased to call 'a highly precarious tenure of Miss Joanna'.

Miss Joanna was a good deal more attractive than her father desired her to be. He took gloomy views of the situation, was disposed to snub any young man who seemed to be casting glances toward his last remaining treasure, and finally announced that when Fate dealt her last and final blow and carried off Johnnie, he should give up the practice of medicine in Burnet, and retire to the High Valley to live as physician in ordinary to the community for the rest of his days. This prospect was so alluring to the married daughters that they turned at once into the veriest match-makers and were disposed to marry Johnnie off immediately—it didn't much matter to whom, so long as they could get possession of their father. Johnnie resented these manoeuvres highly, and obstinately refused to 'remove the impediment', declaring that self-sacrifice was all very well, but she couldn't and wouldn't see that it was her duty to go off and be content with a dull anybody, merely for the sake of giving Papa up to that greedy Clover and Elsie, who had everything in the world already and yet were not content. She liked to be at the head of the Burnet house and rule with a rod of iron, and make Dorry mind his p's and q's; it was much better fun than marrying anyone, and there she was determined to stay, whatever they might say or do. So matters stood at the present time, and though Clover and Elsie still cherished little private plans of their own, nothing, so far, seemed likely to come of them.

Elsie had time to set the room in beautiful order, and Clover had nearly finished her hemming, before the sound of hoofs announced the return of the two husbands from their early ride. They came cantering down the side pass, with appetites sharpened by exercise, and quite ready for the breakfast which Choo Loo presently brought in from the new cooking-cabin, set a little to one side out of sight, in the shelter of the grove. Choo Loo was still a fixture in the valley. He and his methods were a puzzle and somewhat of a distress to the order-loving Clover, who distrusted not a little the ways and means of his mysteriously conducted kitchen; but servants were so hard to come by at the High Valley, and Choo Loo was so steady and faithful and his viands on the whole so good, that she judged it wise to ask no questions and not look too closely into affairs but just take the goods the gods provided, and be thankful that she had any cook at all.

Choo Loo was .an amiable heathen also, and very pleased to serve ladies who appreciated his attempts at decoration, for he had an eye for effect and loved to make things pretty. Clover understood this and never forgot to notice and praise, which gratified Choo Loo, who had found his bachelor employers in the old days somewhat dull and unobservant in this respect.

'Missie like?' he asked this morning, indicating the wreath of wild cranberry vine round the dish of chicken. Then he set a mound of white raspberries in the middle of the table, starred with gold-hearted brown coreopsis, and asked again, 'Missie like dat?' pleased at Clover's answering nod and smile. Noiselessly he came and went on his white-shod feet, fetching in one dish after another, and when all was done, making a sort of dual salaam to the two ladies, and remarking 'Allee yeady now', after which he departed, his pigtail swinging from side to side and his blue cotton garments flapping in the wind as he walked across to the cookhouse.

Delicious breaths of roses and mignonette floated in as the party gathered about the breakfast table. They came from the flower-beds just outside, which Clover sedulously tended, watered, and defended from the roving cattle, which showed a provoking preference for heliotropes over pentstemons whenever they had a chance to get at them.

Cows were a great trial, she considered; and yet after all they were the object of their lives in the Valley, their raison d'etre, and must be put up with accordingly.

'Do you suppose the Youngs have landed yet?' asked Elsie as she qualified her husband's coffee with a dash of thick cream.

'They should have got in last night if the steamer made her usual time. I dare say we shall find a telegram at St. Helen's tomorrow if we go in,' answered her brother-in-law.

'Yes, or possibly Phil will ride out and fetch it. He is always glad of an excuse to come. I wonder what sort of girl Miss Young is. You and Clover never have said much about her.'

'There isn't much to say. She's just an ordinary sort of girl—nice enough and all that, not pretty.'

'Oh Geoff, that's not quite fair. She's rather pretty, that is, she would be if she were not stiff and shy and so very badly dressed. I didn't get on very much with her at Clovelly, but I dare say we shall like her here; and when she limbers out and becomes used to our ways, she'll make a nice neighbour.'

'Dear me, I hope so,' remarked Elsie. 'It's really quite important what sort of a girl Miss Young turns out to be. A stiff person whom you had to see every day would be horrid and spoil everything. The only thing we need, the only possible improvement to the High Valley, would be a few more nice people, just two or three, with pretty little houses, you know, dotted here and there in the side canyons, whom we could ride up to visit, and who would come down to see us, and dine and play whist and dance Virginia reels and "Sally Waters" on Christmas Eve. That would be quite perfect. But I suppose it won't happen till nobody knows how long.'

'I suppose so, too,' said Geoff in a tone of well-simulated sympathy. 'Poor Elsie, spoiling for people! Don't set your heart on them. High Valley isn't at all a likely spot to make a neighbourhood of.'

'A neighbourhood! I should think not! A neighbourhood would be horrid. But if two or three people wanted to come—really nice ones, you know, perfect charmers—surely you and Clare wouldn't have the heart to refuse to sell them building lots?'

'We are exactly a whist quartet now,' said Clarence, patting his wife's shoulder. 'Cheer up, dear. You shall have your perfect charmers when they apply; but meantime changes are risky, and I am quite content with things as they are, and am ready to dance "Sally Waters" with you at any time with pleasure. Might I have the honour now, for instance?'

'Indeed, no! Clover and I have to work like beavers on the Youngs' house. And, Clare, we are quite a complete party in ourselves, as you say; but there are the children to be considered. Geoffy and Phillida will want to play whist one of these days, and where is their quartet to come from?'

'We shall have to consider that point when they are a little nearer the whist age. Here they come now. I hear the nursery door slam. They don't look particularly dejected about their future prospects, I must say.'

Four pairs of eyes turned expectantly toward the staircase, down which there presently came the dearest little pair of children that can be imagined. Clover's boy of three was as big as most people's boys of five, a splendid sturdy little Englishman in build, but with his mother's lovely eyes and skin. Phillida, whose real name was Philippa, was of a more delicate and slender make, with dark brown eyes and a mane of ruddy gold which repeated something of the tawny tints of her father's hair and beard. Down they came hand in hand, little Phil holding tightly to the polished baluster, chattering as they went, like two wood-thrushes.

Neither of them had ever known any other child playmates, and they were devoted to each other and quite happy together. Little Geoff from the first had adopted a protecting attitude toward his smaller cousin, and had borne himself like a gallant little knight in the one adventure of their lives, when a stray coyote, wandering near the house, showed his teeth to the two babies whose nurse had left them alone for a moment, and Geoff, only two then, had caught up a bit of stick and thrown himself in front of Phillida with such a rush and shout that the beast turned and fled, before Roxy and the collies could come to the rescue. The dogs chased the coyote up the ravine down which he had come, and he showed himself no more; but Clover was so proud of her boy's prowess that she never forgot the exploit, and it passed into the family annals for all time.

One wonderful stroke of good luck had befallen the young mothers in their mountain solitude, and that was the possession of Roxy and her mother Euphane. They were sister and niece to good old Debby, who for so many years had presided over Dr. Carr's kitchen; and when they arrived one day in Burnet fresh from the Isle of Man, and announced that they had come out for good to better their fortunes, Debby had at once devoted them to the service of Clover and Elsie. They proved the greatest-possible comfort and help to the High Valley household. The place did not seem lonely to them, used as they were to a still lonelier cabin at the top of a steep moor up which few people ever came. The Colorado wages seemed riches, the liberal comfortable living luxury to them, and they rooted and established themselves, just as Debby had done, into a position of trusted and affectionate helpfulness, which seemed likely to endure. Euphane was housemaid, Roxy nurse; it already seemed as though life could never have gone on without them, and Clover was disposed to emulate Dr. Carr in objecting to 'followers', and in resenting any admiring looks cast by herders at Roxy's rosy English cheeks and pretty blue eyes.

Little Geoff ran to his father's knee, as a matter of course, on arriving at the bottom of the stairs, while Phillida climbed her mother's equally as a matter of course. Safely established there, she began at once to flirt with Clarence, making wide coquettish eyes at him, smiling, and hiding her face to peep out and smile again. He seized one of her dimpled hands and kissed it. She instantly pulled it away, and hid her face again.

"Fair Phillida flouts me,' he said. 'Doesn't baby like Papa a bit? Ah, well, he is going to cry, then.'

He buried his face in his napkin and sobbed ostentatiously.

Phillida, not at all impressed, tugged bravely at the corner of the handkerchief; but when the sobs continued and grew louder, she began to look troubled, and leaning forward suddenly, threw her arms round her father's neck and laid her rose-leaf lips on his forehead. He caught her up rapturously and tossed her high in air, kissing her every time she came down.

'You angel! You little angel! You little dear!' he cried, with a positive dew of pleasure in his eyes. 'Elsie, what have we ever done to deserve such a darling?'

'I really don't know what you have done,' remarked Elsie, coolly; 'but I have done a good deal. I always was meritorious in my way, and deserve the best that is going, even Phillida. She is none too good for me. Come back, baby, to your exemplary parent.'

She rose to recapture the child; but Clarence threw a strong arm about her, still holding Phillida on his shoulder, and the three went waltzing merrily down the room, the little one from her perch accenting the dance time with a series of small shouts. Little Geoff looked up soberly, with his mouth full of raspberries, and remarked, 'Aunty, I didn't ever know that people danced at breakfast.'

'No more did I,' said Elsie, trying in vain to get away from her pirouetting husband.

'No more does any one outside this extraordinary valley of ours,' laughed Geoff. 'Now, partner, if you have finished your fandango, allow me to remind you that there are a hundred and forty head of cattle waiting to be branded in the upper valley, and that Manuel is to meet us there at ten o'clock.'

'And we have the breakfast things to wash, and a whole world to do at the Youngs',' declared Elsie, releasing herself with a final twirl. 'Now, Clare dear, order Marigold and Summer-Savoury, please, to be brought down in half an hour, and tell old Jose that we want him to help and scrub. No, young man, not another turn. These sports are unseemly on such a busy day as this. "Dost thou not suspect my place? Dost thou not suspect my years?" as the immortal W. would say. I am twenty-five—nearly twenty-six—and am not to be whisked about thus.'

Everybody went everywhere on horseback in the High Valley, and the gingham riding-skirts and wide-brimmed hats hung always on the antlers, ready to hand, beside waterproofs and top-coats. Before long the sisters were on their way, their saddle-pockets full of little stores, baskets strapped behind them, and the newly made curtains piled on their laps. The distance was about a mile to the house which Lionel Young and his sister were to inhabit.

It stood in a charming situation on the slope of one of the side canyons, facing the high range and backed by a hillside clothed with pines. In build it was very much such a cabin as the original hut had been—six rooms, all on one floor, the sixth being a kitchen. It was newly completed, and sawdust and fresh shavings were littered freely about the place. Clover's first act was to light a fire in the wide chimney for burning these up.

'It looks bare enough,' she remarked, sweeping away industriously. 'But it will be quite easy to make it pleasant if Imogen Young has any faculty at that sort of thing. I'm sure it's a great deal more promising than the Hut was before Clarence and Geoff and I took hold of it. See, Elsie—this room is done. I think Miss Young will choose it for her bedroom, as it is rather the largest; so you might tack up the dotted curtains here while I sweep the other rooms. And that convolvulus chintz is to cover her dresspegs.'

'What fun a house is!' observed Elsie a moment or two later, between her hammer strokes. 'People who can get a carpenter or upholsterer to help them at any minute really lose a great deal of pleasure. I always adored baby-houses when I was little, and this is the same thing grown up.'

'I don't know,' replied Clover, abstractedly, as she threw a last dustpanful of chips into the fire. 'It is good fun, certainly; but out here one has so much of it that sometimes it comes under the suspicion of being hard work. Now, when Jose has the kitchen windows washed it will all be pretty decent. We can't undertake much beyond making the first day or two more comfortable. Miss Young will prefer to make her own plans and arrangements; and I don't fancy she's the sort of girl who will enjoy being too much helped.'

'Somehow I don't get quite an agreeable idea of Miss Young from what you and Geoffrey say of her. I do hope she isn't going to make herself disagreeable.'

'Oh, I'm sure she won't do that; but there is a wide distance between not being disagreeable and being agreeable. I didn't mean to give you an unpleasant impression of her. In fact, my recollections about her are rather indistinct. We didn't see a great deal of her when we were at Clovelly, or perhaps it was that Isabel and I were out so much and there was so much coming and going.'

'But are not she and Isabel very intimate?'

'I think so; but they are not a bit alike. Isabel is delightful. I wish it were she who was coming out. You would love her. Now, my child, we must begin on the kitchen tins.'

It was an all-day piece of work which they had undertaken, and they had ordered dinner late accordingly, and provided themselves with a basket of sandwiches. By half past five all was fairly in order—the windows washed, the curtains up, kitchen utensils and china unpacked and arranged, and the somewhat scanty supply of furniture placed to the best advantage.

'There! Robinson Crusoe would consider himself in clover; and even Miss Young can exist for a couple of days, I should think,' said Elsie, standing back to note the effect of the last curtain. 'Lionel will have to go in to St. Helen's and get a lot of things out before it will be really comfortable, though. There come the boys now to ride home with us. No, there is only one horse. Why, it is Phil!'

Phil indeed it was, but such a different Phil from the delicate boy whom. Clover had taken out to Colorado six years before. He was now a broad-shouldered, muscular, athletic young fellow, full of life and energy, and showing no trace of the illness which at that time seemed so menacing. He gave a shout when he caught sight of his sisters, and pushed his bronco to a gallop, waving a handful of envelopes high in the air.

'This despatch came last night for Geoff,' he explained, dismounting, 'and there were a lot of letters besides, so I thought I'd better bring them out. I left the newspapers and the rest at the house, and fetched your share on. Euphane told me where you two were. So this is where the Youngs are going to live, is it?'

He stepped in at the door and took a critical survey of the interior, while Clover and Elsie examined their letters.

This telegram is for Geoff,' explained Clover. 'The Youngs are here,' and she read:

Safely landed. We reach Denver Thursday morning, six-thirty.

LIONEL YOUNG.

'So they will get here on Thursday afternoon. It's lucky we came up today. My letters are from Johnnie and Cecy Slack. Johnnie says— —'

Elsie was interrupted by a joyful shriek from Clover, who had torn open her letter and was eagerly reading it.

'Oh Elsie, Elsie, what do you think is going to happen? The most enchanting thing! Rose Red is coming out here in August! She and Mr. Browne and Roslein! Was there ever anything so nice in this world! Just hear what she says:

In the High Valley

BOSTON, June 30.

MY DUCKY-DADDLES AND MY DEAR ELSIE GIRL,I have something so wonderful to tell that I can scarcely find words in which to tell it. A kind Providence and the A.T. and S.F.R.R. have just decided that Deniston must go to New Mexico early in August. This would not have been at all delightful under ordinary circumstances, for it would only have meant perspiration on his part and widowhood on mine, but most fortunately, some angels with a private car of their own have turned up, and have asked all three of us to go out with them as far as Santa Fe. What do you think of that? It is not the Daytons, who seem only to exist

to carry you to and fro from Burnet to Colorado free of expense, this time, but another batch of angels who have to do with the road—name of Hopkinson. I never set eyes on them, but they appear to my imagination equipped with the largest kind of wings and nimbuses round their heads as big as shade-hats.

I have always longed to get out somehow to your Enchanted Valley, and see all your mysterious husbands and babies, and find out for myself what the charm is that makes you so wonderfully contented there, so far from West Cedar Street and the other centres of light and culture, but I never supposed I could come unless I walked. But now I am coming! I do hope none of you have the small-pox, or pleuro-pneumonia, or the 'foot-and-mouth disease' (whatever that is), or any other of the ills to which men and cattle are subject, and which will stand in the way of the visit. Deniston, of course, will be forced to go right through to Santa Fe, but Roslein and I are at your service if you like to have us. We don't care for scenery, we don't want to see Mexico or the Pacific Coast, or the buried cities of Central America, or the Zuni corn dance—if there is such a thing—or any alkaline plains, or pueblos, or buttes, or buffalo wallows; we only want to see you, individually and collectively, and the High Valley. May we come and stay a fortnight? Deniston thinks he shall be gone at least as long as that. We expect to leave Boston on the 3ist of July. You will know what time we ought to get to St. Helen's—I don't, and I don't care, so only we get there and find you at the station. Oh, my dear Clovy, isn't it fun?

I have seen several of our old school-set lately, Esther Dearborn for one. She is Mrs. Joseph P. Allen now, as you know, and has come to live at Chestnut Hill, quite close by. I had never seen her since her marriage, nearly five years since, till the other day, when she asked me out to lunch, and introduced me to Mr. Joseph P., who seems a very nice man, and also—now don't faint utterly, but you will!—to their seven children! He had two of his own when they married, and they have had two pairs of twins since, and 'a singleton', as they say in whist. Such a houseful you never did see; but the twins are lovely, and Esther looks very fat and happy and well-to-do, and says she doesn't mind it a bit, and sees more clearly every day that the thing she was born for was to take the charge of a large family. Her Joseph P. is very well off, too. I should judge that they 'could have cranberry sauce every day and never feel the difference', which an old cousin of my mother's whom I dimly remember as a part of my childhood, used to regard as representing the high-water mark of wealth.

Mary Strothers has been in town lately, too. She has only one child, a little girl, which seems miserably few compared with Esther, but on the other hand she has never been without neuralgia in the face for one moment since she went to live in the Hoosac Tunnel, she told me, so there are compensations. She seems happy for all that, poor dear Mary. Ellen Gray never has married at all, you know. She goes into good works instead, Girls' Friendlies and all sorts of usefulnesses. I do admire her so much, she is a standing reproach and example to me. 'Wish I were a better boy,' as your brother Dorry said in his journal.

Mother is well and my father, but the house seems empty and lonely now. We can never get used to dear grandmamma's loss, and Sylvia is gone too. She and Tom sailed for Europe in April, and it makes a great difference having them away, even for a summer. My brother-in-law is such a nice fellow, I hope you will know him some day.

And all this time I have forgotten to tell you the chief news of all, which is that I have seen Katy. Deniston and I spent Sunday before last with her at the Torpedo Station., She has a cosy, funny little house, one of a row of five or six, built on the spine, so to speak, of a narrow, steep island, with a beautiful view of Newport just across the water. It was a superb day, all shimmery blue and gold, and we spent most of our time sitting in a shady corner of the piazza, and talking of the old times and of all of you. I didn't know then of this enchanting Western plan, or we should have had a great deal more to talk about. The dear Katy looks very well and handsome, and was perfectly dear, as she always is, and she says the Newport climate suits her to perfection. Your brother-in-law is a stunner! I asked Katy if she wasn't going out to see you soon and she said not till Ned went to sea next spring, then she should go for a long visit.

Write at once if we may come. I won't begin on the subject of Roslein, whom you will never know, she has grown so. She goes about saying rapturously, 'I shall see little Geoff! I shall see Phillida! I shall see Aunt Clovy! Perhaps I shall ride on a horse!' You'll never have the heart to disappoint her. My 'milk teeth are chattering with fright' at the idea of so much railroad, as one of her books says, but for all that we are coming, if you let us. Do let us!

Your own ROSE RED.

'Let them! I should think so,' cried Clover, with a little skip of rapture. 'Dear, dear Rose! Elsie, the nicest sort of things do happen out here, don't they?'

CHAPTER FIVE : ARRIVAL

The train from Denver was nearing St. Helen's —and Imogen Young looked eagerly from the window for a first sight of the place. Their journey had been exhaustingly hot during its last stages, the alkaline dust most trying, and they had had a brief experience of a sand-storm on the plains, which gave her a new idea as to what wind and grit can accomplish in the way of discomfort. She was very tired, and quite disposed to be critical and unenthusiastic; still she had been compelled to admit that the run down from Denver lay over an interesting country.The town on its plateau was shining in full sunshine, as it had done when Clover landed there six years before, but its outlines had greatly changed with the increase of buildings.

The mountain range opposite was darkly blue from the shadows of a heavy thunder gust which was slowly rolling away southward. The plains between were of tawny yellow, but the belts of mesa above showed the richest green, except where the lines of alfalfa and grain were broken by white patches of mentzelia and poppies. It was wonderfully beautiful, but the town itself looked so much larger than Imogen had expected that she exclaimed with surprise:

'Why, Lion, it's a city! You said you were bringing me out to live in the wilderness. What made you tell such stories? It looks bigger than Bideford.'

'It looks larger than it did when I came away,' replied her brother. 'Two, three, six—eight fine new houses on

Monument Avenue, by Jove, and any number off there toward the north. You've no idea how these Western places sprout and thrive. Moggy. This isn't twenty years old yet.'

'I can't believe it. You are imposing on me. And why on earth did you let me bring out all those pins and things? There seem to be any number of shops.'

'I let you! Oh, I say, that's good! Why, Moggy, don't you remember how I remonstrated straight through your packing. Never a bit would you listen to me, and here is the result,' pulling out a baggage memorandum as he spoke, and reading aloud in a lugubrious tone, 'Extra weight of trunks, thirteen dollars, fifty-two cents.'

'Thirteen-fifty,' cried Imogen with a gasp. 'My gracious! Why, that's nearly three pounds. Lion! Lion! You ought to have made me listen.'

'I'm sure I did all I could in that way. But cheer up! You'll want your pins yet. You mustn't confound this place with High Valley. That's sixteen miles off and hasn't a shop.'

The discussion was brought to end by the stopping of the train. In another moment Geoff Templestowe appeared at the door.

'Hallo, Lion! Glad to see you. Imogen,' shaking hands warmly, 'how are you? Welcome to Colorado. I'm afraid you've had a bad journey in this heat.'

'It has been beastly. Poor Moggy's dead beat, I'm afraid. Neither of us could sleep a wink last night for the dust and sand. Well, it's all well that ends well. We'll cool her off in the valley. How is everything going on there? Mrs. Templestowe all right, and Mrs. Page, and the children? I declare,' stretching himself, 'it's a blessing to get a breath of good air again.

There's nothing in the world that can compare with Colorado.'

A light carry-all was waiting near the station, whose top was little more than a fringed awning. Into this Geoffrey helped Imogen, and proceeded to settle her wraps and bags in various seat boxes and pockets with which the carriage was cleverly fitted up. It was truly a carry-all and came and went continually between the valley and St. Helen's.

'Now,' he remarked as he stuffed in the last parcel, 'we will just stop long enough to get the mail and some iced tea, which I ordered as I came down, and then be off. You'll find a cold chicken in that basket, Lion. Clover was sure you'd need something, and there's no time for a regular meal if we are to get in before dark.'

'Iced tea! What a queer idea!' said Imogen.

'I forgot that you were not used to it. We drink it a great deal here in summer. Would you rather have some hot? I didn't fancy that you would care for it, the day is so warm; but we'll wait and have it made, if you prefer.'

'Oh, no. I won't delay you,' said Imogen, rather grudgingly. She was disposed to resent the iced tea as an American innovation, but when she tried it she found herself, to her own surprise, liking it very much.

'Only, why do they call it tea?' she meditated. 'It's a great deal more like punch—all lemon and things.' But she had to own that it was wonderfully refreshing.

The sun was blazing on the plain; but after they began to wind up the pass a cool, strong wind blew in their faces and the day seemed suddenly delightful. The unfamiliar flowers and shrubs, the strange rock forms and colours, the occasional mountain glimpses, interested Imogen so much that for a time she forgot her fatigue. Then an irresistible drowsiness seized her; the talk going on between Geoffrey Templestowe and her brother, about cows and feed and the prospect of the autumn sales, became an indistinguishable hum, and she went off into a series of sleeps broken by brief wakings,. when the carry-all bumped, or swayed heavily from side to side on the steep inclines. From one of the soundest of these naps she was roused by her brother shaking her arm and calling:

'Moggy, wake, wake up! We are here.'

With a sharp thump of heart-beat she started into full consciousness to find the horses-drawing up before a deep vine-hung porch, on which stood a group of figures which seemed to her confused senses a large party. There was Elsie in a fresh white dress with pale green ribbons, Clarence Page, Phil Carr, little Philippa in her nurse's arms, small Geoff with his two collies at his side, and foremost of all, ready to help her down, hospitable little Clover, in lilac muslin, with a rose in her belt and a face of welcome.

'How the Americans do love dress!' was Imogen's instant thought— an ungracious one, and quite unwarranted by the circumstances. Clover and Elsie kept themselves neat and pretty from habit and instinct, but the muslin gowns were neither new nor fashionable, they had only the merit of being fresh and becoming to their wearers.

'You poor child, how tired you must be!' cried Clover, as she assisted Imogen out of the carriage. 'This is my sister, Mrs. Page. Please take Miss Young directly to her room, Elsie, while I order up some hot water. She'll be glad of that first of all. Lion, I won't take time to welcome you now. The boys must care for you while I see after your sister.'

A big sponging-bath full of fresh water stood ready in the room to which Imogen was conducted; the white bed was invitingly 'turned down'; there were fresh flowers on the dressing-table, and a heap of soft cushions on a roomy divan which filled the deep recess of a range of low windows. The gay-flowered paper on the walls ran up to the peak of the ceiling, giving a tent-like effect. Most of the furnishings were home-made. The divan was nothing more or less than a big packing-box nicely stuffed and upholstered; the dressing-table, a construction of pine boards covered and frilled with cretonne. Clover had plaited the chintz round the looking-glass and on the edges of the book-shelves, while the picture-frames, the comer-brackets, and the impromptu washstand owed their existence to Geoff's cleverness with tools. But the whole effect was pretty and tasteful, and Imogen, as she went on with her dressing, looked about her with a somewhat reluctant admiration, which was slightly tinctured with dismay.

I suppose they got all these things out from the East,' she reflected. 'I couldn't undertake them in our little cabin, I'm sure. It's very nice, and really in very good taste, but it must have cost a great deal. The Americans don't think of that, however; and I've always heard they have a great knack at doing up their houses and making a good show.'

'Go straight to bed if you feel like it. Don't think of coming down. We will send you up some dinner,' Clover had urged; but Imogen, tired as she was, elected to go down.'I really mustn't give in to a little fatigue,' she thought..'I have the honour of England to sustain over here.' So she heroically put on her heavy tweed travelling-dress again, and descended the stairs, to find a bright little fire of pinewood and cones snapping and blazing on the hearth, and the whole party gathered about it, waiting for her and dinner.

'What an extraordinary climate!' she exclaimed in a tone of astonishment. 'Melting with heat at three, and here at a quarter past seven you are sitting round a fire! It really feels comfortable, too!'

'The changes are very sharp,' said Geoff, rising to give her his chair. 'Such a daily drop in temperature would make a sensation in our good old Devonshire, would it not? You see it comes from the high elevation. We are nearly eight thousand feet above the sea-level here; that is about twice as high as the top of the highest mountain in the United Kingdom.'

'Fancy! I had no idea of it. Lionel did say something about the elevation, but I didn't clearly attend.' She glanced about the room, which was looking its best, with the pink light of the shaded candles falling on the white-spread table, and the flickering fire making golden glows and gleams on the ceiling. 'How did you get all these pretty things out here?' she suddenly demanded.'Some came in wagons, and some just "growed",' explained Clover, merrily. 'We will let you into our secrets gradually. Ah, here comes dinner at last, and I am sure we shall all be glad of it.'

Choo Loo now entered with the soup-tureen, a startling vision to Imogen, who had never seen a Chinaman before in her life.

'How very extraordinary!' she murmured in an aside to Lionel. 'He looks like an absolute heathen. Are such things usual here?'

'Very usual, I should say. Lots of them about. That fellow has a Joss in his cabin, and very likely a prayer-wheel; but he's a capital cook. I wish we could have the luck to happen on his brother or nephew for ourselves.'

'I don't, then,' replied his scandalized sister. 'I can't feel that it is right to employ such people in a Christian country. The Americans have such lax notions!'

'Hold up a bit! What do you know about their notions? Nothing at all.'

'Come to dinner,' said Clover's pleasant voice. 'Geoff, Miss Young will sit next to you. Put a cushion behind her back, Clarence.'

Dinner over, Imogen concluded that she had upheld the honour of England quite as long as was desirable, or in fact possible, and gladly accepted permission to go at once to bed. She was fairly tired out.

She woke wonderfully restored by nine hours' solid sleep in that elastic and life-giving atmosphere, and went

downstairs to find everyone scattered to their different tasks and avocations, except Elsie, who was waiting to pour her coffee. Clover and Lionel were gone to the new house, she explained, and they were to follow them as soon as Imogen had breakfasted.

Elsie's manner lacked its usual warmth and ease. She had taken no fancy at all to the stiff, awkward little English woman, in whom her quick wits detected the lurking tendency to cavil and criticize, and was discouraging accordingly. Oddly enough, Imogen liked this offish manner of Elsie's. She set it down to a proper sense of decorum and retenue. 'So different from the usual American gush and making believe to be at ease always with everybody,' she thought; and she made herself as agreeable as possible to Elsie, whom she considered much prettier than Clover, and in every way more desirable. These impressions were doubtless tinctured by the underlying jealousy from which she had so long suffered, and which still influenced her, though Isabel Templestowe was now far away, and there was no one at hand to be jealous about.

The two rode amicably up the valley together.

'There, that's your new home,' said Elsie, when they came in sight of the just finished cabin. 'Didn't Lionel choose a pretty site for it? And you have a most beautiful view.'

'Well, Moggy,' cried her brother, hurrying out to help her dismount, 'here you are at last. Mrs. Templestowe and I have made you a fire and done all sorts of things. How do you like the look of it? It's a decent little place, isn't it? We must get Mrs. Templestowe to put us up to some of her nice little dodges about furniture and so on, such as they have at the other house. She and Mrs. Page have made it all tidy for us, and put up lots of nice little curtains and things. They must have worked awfully hard, too. Wasn't it good of them?'

'Very,' said Imogen, rather stiffly. 'I'm sure we're much obliged to you, Mrs. Templestowe. I fear you have given yourself a great deal of trouble.'

The words were polite enough, but the tone was distinctly repellent.

'Oh, no,' said Clover, lightly. 'It was only fun to come up and arrange a little beforehand. We were very glad to do it. Now, Elsie, you and I will ride down and leave these new housekeepers to discuss their plans in peace. Dinner at six tonight, Lionel; and please send old Jose down if you need anything. Don't stay too long or get too tired, Miss Young. We shall have lunch about one; but if you are doing anything and don't want to leave so early, you'll find some sardines and jam and a tin of biscuits in the cupboard by the fire.'

She and Elsie rode away accordingly. When they were out of hearing, Clover remarked:

'I wonder why that girl dislikes me so.'

'Dislikes you! Clover, what do you mean? Nobody ever disliked you in your life, or ever could.'

'Yes, she does,' persisted Clover. 'She has got some sort of queer twist in her mind regarding me, and I can't think what it is. It doesn't really matter, and very likely she'll get over it presently; but I'm sorry about it. It would be so pleasant all to be good friends together up here, where there are so few of us.'

Her tone was a little pathetic. Clover was used to being liked.

'Little wretch!' cried Elsie, with flashing eyes. 'If I really thought that she dared not to like you, I'd—I'd—well, what would I do?— import a grizzly bear to eat her, or some such thing! I suppose an Indian could be found who for a consideration would undertake to scalp Miss Imogen Young, and if she doesn't behave herself he shall be found. But you're all mistaken, Clovy; you must be. She's only stiff and dull and horribly English, and very tired after her journey. She'll be all right in a day or two. If she isn't, I shall "go for" her without mercy.'

'Well, perhaps it is that.' It was easier and pleasanter to imagine Imogen tired than to admit that she was absolutely unfriendly.

'After all,' she added, 'it's for Miss Young's sake that I should regret it if it were so, much more than for my own. I have Geoff and you and Clare—and Papa and Johnnie coming, and dear Rose Red—all of you are at my back; but she, poor thing, has no one but Lionel to stand up for her. I am on my own ground,' drawing up her figure with a pretty movement of pride, 'and she is a stranger in a strange land. So we won't mind if she is stiff, Elsie dear, and just be as nice as we can to her, for it must be horrid to be so far away from home and one's own people. We cannot be too patient and considerate under such circumstances.'

Meanwhile the moment they were out of sight Lionel had turned upon his sister sharply, and angrily.

'Moggy, what on earth do you mean by speaking so to Mrs. Templestowe?'

'Speaking how? What did I say?' retorted Imogen.

'You didn't say anything out of the common, but your manner was most disagreeable. If she hadn't been the best-tempered woman in the world she would have resented it on the spot. Here she, and all of them, have been doing all they can to make ready for us, giving us such a warm welcome too, treating us as if we were their own kith and kin, and you return it by putting on airs as if she were intruding and interfering in our affairs. I never was so ashamed of a member of my own family before in my life.'

'I can't imagine what you mean,' protested Imogen, not quite truthfully. 'And you've no call to speak to me so,

Lionel, and tell me I am rude, just because I don't gush and go about making cordial speeches like these Americans of yours. I'm sure I said everything that was proper to Mrs. Templestowe.'

'Your words were proper enough, but your manner was eminently improper. Now Moggy,' changing his tone,

'listen to me. Let us look the thing squarely in the face. You've come out here with me, and it's awfully good of you and I shan't ever forget it; but here we are, settled for years to come in this little valley, with the Templestowes and Pages for our only neighbours. They can be excellent friends, as I've found, and they are prepared to be equally friendly to you; but if you're going to start with a little grudge against Mrs. Geoff—who's the best little woman going, by Jove, and the kindest—you'll set the whole family against us, and we might as well pack up our traps at once and go back to England. Now I put it to you reasonably; is it worth while to upset all our plans and all my hopes—and for what? Mrs. Templestowe can't have done anything to set you against her?'

'Lion,' cried Imogen, bursting into tears, 'don't! I'm sure I didn't mean to be rude. Mrs. Geoff never did anything to displease me, and certainly I haven't a grudge against her. But I'm very tired, so please don't s-c-o-l-d me; I've got no one out here but you.'

Lionel melted at once. He had never seen his sister cry before, and felt that he must have been harsh and unkind.

'I'm a brute,' he exclaimed. 'There, Moggy, there, dear—don't cry. Of course you're tired; I ought to have thought of it before.'

He petted and consoled her, and Imogen, who was really spent and weary, found the process so agreeable that she prolonged her tears a little. At last she suffered herself to be comforted, dried her eyes, grew cheerful, and the two proceeded to make an investigation of the premises, deciding what should go there and what here, and what it was requisite to get from St. Helen's. Imogen had to own that the ladies of the Valley had been both thoughtful and helpful.

'I'll thank them again this evening and do it better,' she said; and Lionel patted her back, and told her she really was quite a little brick when she wasn't a big goose—a brotherly compliment which was more gratifying than it sounded.

It was decided that he should go into St. Helen's next day to order out stores and what Lionel called 'a few sticks' that were essential, and procure a servant.

'Then we can move in the next day,' said Imogen. 'I feel in such a hurry to begin housekeeping, Lionel, you can't think. One is always a stranger in the land till one has a place of one's own. Geoff and his wife are very kind and polite, but it's much better we should start for ourselves as soon as possible. Besides, there are other people coming to stay; Mrs. Page said so.'

'Yes, but not for quite a bit yet, I fancy. All the same, you are right, Moggy; and we'll set up our own shebang as soon as it can be managed. You'll feel twice as much at home when you have a house of your own. I'll get the mattresses and tables and chairs out by Saturday, and fetch the slavey out with me if I can find one.'

'No Chinese need apply,' said Imogen. 'Get me a Christian servant, whatever you do, Lion. I can't bear that creature with the pigtail.'

'I'll do my possible,' said her brother, in a doubtful tone; 'but you'll come to pigtails yet and be thankful for them, or I miss my guess.'

'Never!'

Imogen remembered her promise. She was studiously polite and grateful that evening, said exerted herself to talk and undo the unpleasant impression of the morning. The little party round the dinner-table waxed merry, especially when Imogen, under the effect of her gracious resolves, attempted to adapt her conversation to her company and gratify her hosts by using American expressions.

'People absquatulate from St. Helen's toward autumn, don't they?' she remarked. Then when someone laughed she added, 'You say "absquatulate" over here, don't you?'

'Well, I don't know. I never did hear anyone say it except as a joke,' replied Elsie.

And again: 'Mother would be astonished, Lion, wouldn't she, if she knew that Chinese can make English puddings as well as the cooks at home. She'd be all struck of a heap.'

And later: 'It really was dreadful. The train was broken all to bits, and nearly everyone on board was hurt—

catawampously chawed up in fact, as you Americans would say. Why, what are you laughing at? Don't you say it?'

'Never, except in the comic newspapers and dime novels,' said Geoffrey Templestowe when he recovered from his amusement, while Lionel utterly overcome with his sister's vocabulary, choked and strangled, and finally found voice to say:

'Go on, Moggy. You're doing beautifully. Nothing like acquiring the native dialect to make a favourable impression in a new country. Oh, wherever did she learn "catawampous"? I shall die of it.'

CHAPTER SIX : UNEXPECTED

Imogen's race-prejudices experienced a weakening after Lionel's return from St. Helen's with the only 'slavey' attainable, in the shape of an untidy, middle-aged Irish woman, with red hair, and a hot little spark of temper glowing in either eye. Putting this unpromising female in possession of the fresh, clean kitchen of the cabin was a trial, but it had to be done; and the young mistress, with all the ardour of inexperience, bent herself to the task of reformation and improvement, and teaching Katty Malony—who was old enough to be her mother—a great many desirable things which she herself did not very well understand. It was thankless work and resulted as such experiments do. Katty gave warning at the end of a week, affirming that she wasn't going to be hectored and driven round by a bit of a miss, who didn't well know what she wanted; and that the Valley was that lonesome anyhow that she'd not remain in it; no, not if the Saints themselves came down from glory and kivered up every fut of soil with shining gold, and she a-starving in the mud—that she wouldn't!

Imogen saw her go with small regret. She had no idea how difficult it might be to find a successor, and it was not till three incompetents of the same nationality had been lured out by the promise of high wages, only to decide that the place was too 'lonely' for them and incontinently depart, that she realized how hard was the problem of 'help' in such a place. It was her first trial at independent housekeeping, and with her English ideas she had counted on neatness, respectfulness of manner, and a certain amount of training as a matter of course in a servant. One has to learn one's way in a new country by the hardest, and perhaps the least hard parts of Imogen's lesson were the intervals when she and Lionel did the work themselves, with only old Jose to scrub and wash up; then at least they could be quiet and at peace, without daily controversies. Later, relief and comfort came to them in the shape of a gentle Mongolian named Ah Lee, procured through the good offices of Choo Loo, whom Imogen was only too thankful to accept, pigtail and all, for his gentleness of manner, general neatness and capacity, and the good taste which he gave to his dishes. In fact, she confessed one day to Lionel, privately in a moment of confidence, that rather than lose him, she would herself carve a joss stick and nail it up in the kitchen; which concession proves the liberalizing and widening effect of necessity upon the human mind. But this is anticipating.

The cabin was a pleasant place enough when once fairly in order. There was an abundance of sunshine, firewood was plentiful, and so small a space was easily kept tidy. Imogen, when she reviewed her resources, realized how wise Lionel had been in recommending her to bring more ornamental things and fewer articles of mere use, such as tapes and buttons. Buttons and tapes were easy enough to come by; but things to make the house pretty were difficult to obtain and cost a great deal. She made the most of her few possessions, and supplied what was lacking with wild flowers, which could be had in any quantity for the picking. Lionel had hunted a good deal during his first Colorado years, and possessed quite a good supply of fox, wolf, and bear skins. These did duty for rugs on the floor. Elk and buffalo horns fastened on the walls served as pegs on which to hang whips and hats. Some gay Mexican pots adorned the chimney-piece; it all looked pretty enough and quite comfortable. Imogen would fain have tried her hand at home-made devices of the sort in which the ladies at the lower house excelled, but somehow her attempts turned out failures. She lacked lightness of touch and originality of fancy, and the results were apt to be what Elsie privately stigmatized as 'wapses of red flannel and burlaps without form or comeliness', at which Lionel jeered, while visitors discreetly averted their eyes lest they should be forced to express an opinion concerning them.

Imogen's views as to the character and capacities of American women underwent many modifications during that first summer in the Valley. It seemed to her that Mrs. Temple-stowe and her sister were equal to any emergency however sudden and unexpected. She was filled with daily wonder over their knowledge of practical details, and their extraordinary 'handiness'. If a herder met with an accident they seemed to know just what to do. If Choo Loo was taken with a cramp or some odd Chinese disease without a name, and laid aside for a day or two, Clover not only nursed him but went into the kitchen as a matter of course, and extemporized a meal which was sufficiently satisfactory for all concerned. If a guest arrived unexpectedly they were not put out; if some article of daily supply failed, they seemed always to devise a substitute; and through all and every contingency they managed to look pretty and bright and gracious, and make sunshine in the shadiest places.

Slowly, for Imogen's mind was not of the quick working order, she took all this in, and her respect for America and Americans rose accordingly. She was forced to own that whatever the rest of womankind in this extraordinary new country might be, these particular specimens were of a sort which any land, even England, might be justly proud to claim.

'And with all they do, they contrive to look so nice,' she said to herself. 'I can't understand how they manage it. Their gowns fit so well, and they always seem to have just the right kind of thing to put on. It is really wonderful, and it certainly isn't because they think a great deal about it. Before I came over I always imagined that American women spent their time in reading fashion magazines and talking over their clothes. Mrs. Geoff and Mrs. Page certainly don't do that. I don't often hear them speak about dresses, or see them at work at them; and both of them know a great deal more about a house than I do, or any other English girl I ever saw. Mrs. Geoff, and Mrs. Page too, can make all sorts of things—cakes and puddings and muffins and even bread; and they read a good deal as well. The Americans are certainly a cleverer people than I supposed.'

The mile of distance between what Clarence called 'the Hut and the Hutlet' counted for little, and a daily intercourse went on, trending chiefly, it must be owned, from the Hut to the Hutlet. Clover was unwearied in small helps and kindnesses. If Imogen were cookless, old Jose was sure to appear with a loaf of freshly baked bread, or a basket of graham gems; or Geoff with a creel of trout and an urgent invitation to lunch or dinner or both. New books made their appearance from below, newspapers and magazines; and if ever the day came when Imogen felt hopelessly faint-hearted, lonely, and over-worked, she was sure to see the flutter of skirts, and her pretty, cordial neighbours would come riding up the trail to cheer her, and to propose something pleasant or helpful. Sometimes Elsie would have her baby on her knee, trusting to 'Summer Savory's' sure-footed steadiness; sometimes little Geoff would be riding beside his mother on a minute burro. Always it seemed as though they brought the sun with them; and she learned to watch for their coming on dull days, as if they were in the secret of her moods and knew just when they were most wanted. But they came so often that these coincidences were not so wonderful, after all.

Imogen did appreciate all this kindness, and was grateful, and, after her manner, responsive; still the process of what Elsie termed 'limbering out Miss Young' went on but slowly. The English stock, firm-set and sturdily rooted, does not 'limber' readily, and a bent toward prejudice is never easily shaken. Compelled to admit that Clover was worth liking, compelled to own her good nature and friendliness, Imogen yet could not be cordially at ease with her. Always an inward stiffness made itself apparent when they were together, and always Clover was aware of the fact. It made no difference in her acts of goodwill, but it made some difference in the pleasure with which she did them— though on no account would she have confessed it, especially to Elsie, who was so comically ready to fire up and offer battle if she suspected anyone of undervaluing her sister. So the month of July went.

It was on the morning of the last day, when the long summer had reached its height of ripeness and completeness, and all things seemed making themselves ready for Rose Red, who was expected in three days more, that Clover, sitting with her work on the shaded western piazza, saw the unwonted spectacle of a carriage slowly mounting the steep road up the Valley. It was so unusual to see any wheeled vehicle there, except their own carry-all, that it caused a universal excitement. Elsie ran to the window overhead with Phillida in her arms; little Geoff stood on the porch staring out of a pair of astonished eyes, and Clover came forward to meet the new arrivals with an unmistakable look of surprise in her face. The gentleman who was driving and the lady beside him were quite unknown to her; but from the back part of the carriage a head extended itself—an elderly head, with a bang of oddly frizzled grey hair and a pair of watery blue eyes, all surmounted by an eccentric shade hat, and all beaming and twittering with recognition and excitement. It took Clover a moment to disentangle her ideas; then she perceived that it was Mrs. Watson, who, when she and Phil first came out to Colorado, years before, came with them, and for a time had been one of the chief trials and perplexities of their life there.

'Well, my dear, and I don't wonder that you look astonished, for no one would suppose that after all I went through with I should ever again —This is my daughter, and her husband, you know, and of course their coming made it seem quite—We are staying in the Ute Valley; only five miles over, they said it was, but such miles! I'd rather ride ten on a level, any day, as I told Ellen, and—well, they said you were living up here; and though the road was pretty rough, it was possible to—And if ever there was a man who could drive a buggy up to the moon, as Ellen declares, Henry is the—but really I was hardly prepared for—but anyway we started, and here we are! What a wild sort of place it is that you are living in, my dear Miss Carr— not that I ought to call you Miss Carr, for—I got your cards, of course, and I was told then that—And your sister marrying the other young man and coming out to live here too! That must be very—Oh, dear me! Is that little boy yours? Well, I never!'

'I am very glad to see you, I am sure,' said Clover, taking the first opportunity of a break in the torrent of words, 'and Mrs. Phillips too— this is Mrs. Phillips, is it not? Let me help you out, Mrs. Watson, and Geoffy dear, run round to the other door and ask Euphane to send somebody to take the horses.'

'Thank you,' said Mrs. Phillips. 'Let me introduce my husband, Mrs. Templestowe. We are at the hotel in the Ute Valley for three days, and my mother wished so much to drive over and see you that we have brought her. What a beautiful place your valley is!'

Mrs. Phillips, tall, large-featured, dark and rather angular, with a pleasant, resolute face, and a clear-cut, rather incisive way of speaking, offered as complete a contrast to her pale, pudgy, incoherent little mother as could well be imagined. Clover's instant thought was, 'Now I know what Mr. Watson must have been like.' Mr. Phillips was also tall, with a keen, Roman-nosed face, and eyeglasses. Both had the look of people who knew what was what and had seen the world—just the sort of persons, it would seem, to whom a parent like Mrs. Watson would be a great trial; and it was the more to their credit that they never seemed in the least impatient, and were evidently devoted to her comfort in all ways. If she fretted them, as she undoubtedly must, they gave no sign of it, and were outwardly all affectionate consideration.

'Why, where is your little boy gone? I wanted to see him,' said Mrs. Watson, as soon as she was safely out of the carriage. 'He was here just this moment, and then—I must say you have got a beautiful situation; and if mountains were all that one needed to satisfy—but I recollect how you used to go on about them at St. Helen's —Take care, Ellen, your skirt is caught! Ah, that's right! Miss Carr is always so—but I mustn't call her that, I know, only I never— And now, my dear, I must have a kiss, after climbing up all this way; and there were gopher holes—at least, a man we met said they were that, and I really thought—Tell me how you are, and all about—That's right, Henry, take out the wraps; you never can tell how—Of course Miss Carr's people are all—I keep calling you Miss Carr; I really can't help it. What a beautiful view!'

Clover now led the way indoors. The central room, large, cool and flower-scented, was a surprise to the eastern guests, who were not prepared to find anything so pretty and tasteful in so remote a spot.

'This is really charming!' said Mr. Phillips, glancing from fireplace to wall, and from wall to window; while his wife exclaimed with delight over the Mariposa lilies which filled a glass bowl on the table, and the tall sheaves of scarlet pentstemons on either side the hearth. Mrs. Watson blinked about curiously, actually silent for a moment, before her surprise took the form of words.

'Why, how pretty it looks, doesn't it, Ellen? And so large and spacious, and so many— I'm all the more surprised because when we were together before, you wouldn't go to the Shoshone House, you remember, because it was so expensive, and of course I—well, circumstances do alter; and it is a world of changes, as Dr. Billings said in one of his sermons last spring. And I'm sure I'm glad, only I wasn't prepared to—Ellen! Ellen! Look at that etching! It's exactly the same as yours, which, Jane Phillips gave you and Henry for your tin wedding. It was very expensive, I know, for I was with her when she got it, and so—at Doll's it was; and his things naturally—but I really think the frame of this is the handsomest! Now, my dear Miss Carr, where did you get that?'

'It was one of our gifts,' said Clover, smiling. 'There is a double supply of wedding presents in this house, Mrs. Watson, for my sister's are here as well as our own. So we are rather rich in pretty things, as you see, but not in anything else, except cows; of those we have any number. Now, if you will all excuse me for a moment, I will go up and tell Mrs. Page that you are here.'

Up she went, deliberately till she was out of sight, and then at a swift, light run the rest of the way.

'Elsie dear,' she cried, bursting into the nursery, 'who do you think is here? Mrs. Watson, our Old Woman of the Sea, you know. She has her son-in-law and daughter with her, and they look like rather nice people, strange to say. They have driven over from the Ute Valley, and of course they must have some lunch; but as it happens it is the worst day of the whole year for them to choose, for I have sent Choo Loo into St. Helen's to look up a Chinese cook for Imogen Young, and I meant to starve you all on poached eggs and raspberries for lunch. I can't leave them of course, but will you just run down, my darling duck, and see what can be done, and tell Euphane? There are cans of soup, of course, and sardines, and all that, but I fear the bread supply is rather short. I'll take Phillida. She's as neat as a new pin, happily. Ah, there's Geoffy. Come and have your hair brushed, boy.'

She went down with one child in her arms and the other holding her hand—a pretty little picture for those below.

'My sister will come presently,' she explained. 'This is her little girl. And here is my son, Mrs. Watson.'

'Dear me—I had no idea he was such a big child,' said that lady. 'Five years old, is he, or six? Only three! Oh yes, what am I thinking about; of course he—Well, my little man, and how do you like living up here in this lonesome place?'

'Very much,' replied little Geoff, backing away from the questioner, as she aimlessly reached out after him.

'He has never lived anywhere else,' Clover explained; 'so he cannot make comparisons. Ignorance is bliss, we are told, Mrs. Watson.'

Euphane, staid and respectable in her spotless apron, now entered with the lunch-cloth, and Clover convoyed her guests upstairs to refresh themselves with cold water after the dust of the drive. By the time they returned the table was set, and presently Elsie appeared, cool and fresh in her pretty pink and white gingham with a knot of rose-coloured ribbon in her wavy hair, her cheeks deepened to just the becoming tint, the very picture of a dainty, well-cared-for little lady. No one would have suspected that during the last half-hour she had stirred and baked a pan of brown 'gems', mixed a cream mayonnaise for the lettuce, set a glass dish of 'junket' to form, and skimmed two pans of cream, beside getting out the soup and sweets for

Euphane, and trimming the dishes of fruit with kinnikinnick and coreopsis. The little feast seemed to have got itself ready in some mysterious manner, without trouble to anyone, which is the last added grace of any feast.

'It is perfectly charming here,' said Mrs. Phillips, more and more impressed. 'I have seen nothing at all like this at the West.'

'There isn't any other place exactly like our valley, I really think. Of course there are other natural parks among the ranges of the Rockies, but ours always seems to me quite by itself. You see we lie so as to catch the sun, and it makes a great difference even in the winter. We have done very little to the Valley, beyond just making ourselves comfortable.'

'Very comfortable indeed, I should say.'

'And so you married the other young man, my dear?' Mrs. Watson was remarking to Elsie. I remember he used to come in very often to call on your sister, and it was easy enough to see—people in boarding-houses will notice such things of course, and we all used to think— But there—of course she knew all the time, and it is easy to make mistakes, and I dare say it's all for the best as it is. You look very young indeed to be married. I wonder that your father could make up his mind to let you.'

'I am not young at all, I'm nearly twenty-six,' replied Elsie, who always resented remarks about her youth. 'There are three younger than I am in the family, and they are all grown up.'

'Oh, my dear, but you don't look it! You don't seem a day over twenty. Ellen was nearly as old as you are before she ever met Henry, and they were engaged nearly two—But she never did look as young as most of the girls she used to go with, and I suppose that's the reason that now they are all got on a little, she seems younger than—Well, well! We never thought while I was with your sister at St. Helen's, helping to take care of your poor brother, you know, how it would all turn out. There was a young man who used to bring roses—I forget his name, and one day Mrs. Gibson said— Her husband had weak lungs and they came out to Colorado on that account, but I believe he—They were talking of building a house, and I meant to ask—But there, I forgot; one does grow so forgetful if one travels much and sees a good many people; but as I was saying—he got well, I think.'

'Who, Mr. Gibson?' asked Elsie, quite bewildered.

'Oh, no! Not Mr. Gibson, of course. He died, and Mrs. Gibson married again. Some man she met out at St. Helen's, I believe it was, and I heard that her children didn't like it; but he was rich, I believe and of course—Riches have wings—you know that proverb of course—but it makes a good deal of difference whether they fly toward you or away from you.'

'Indeed it does,' said Elsie, much amused. 'But you asked me if somebody got well. Who was it?'

'Why, your brother of course, He didn't die, did he?'

'Oh dear, no! He is living at St. Helen's now, and perfectly well and strong.'

'Well, that must be a great comfort to you all. I never did think that he was as ill as your sister fancied he was. Girls will get anxious, and when people haven't had a great deal of experience they—He used to laugh a great deal too, and when people do that it seems to me that their lungs—But of course it was only natural at her age. I used to cheer her up all I could and say—-The air is splendid there, of course, and the sun somehow never seems to heat you as it does at the East, though it is hot, but I think when people have weak chests they'd better—Dr. Hope doesn't think so, I know, but after all there are a great many doctors beside Dr. Hope and—Ellen quite agrees with me—What was I saying?'

Elsie wondered on what fragment of the medley she would fix. She was destined never to know, for just then came a trample of hoofs and the 'boys' rode up to the door.

She went out on the porch to meet them and break the news of the unexpected guests.

'That old thing!' cried Clarence, with unflattering emphasis. 'Oh thunder! I thought we were safe from that sort of bore up here. I shall just cut down to the back and take a bite in the barn.'

'Indeed you will do nothing of the sort. Do you suppose I came up to this place, where company only arrives twice a year or so, to be that lonesome thing a cowboy's bride, that you might slip away and take bites in barns? No, sir —not at all. You will please go upstairs, make yourself fit to be seen, and come down and be as polite as possible. Do you hear, Clare?'

She hooked one white finger in his buttonhole, and stood looking in his face with a saucy gaze.

Clarence yielded at once. His small despot knew very well how to rule him and to put down such short-lived attempts at insubordination as he occasionally indulged in.

'All right, Elsie, I'll go if I must. They're not to stay the night, are they?'

'Heaven forbid! No indeed, they are going back to the Ute Valley.'

He vanished, and presently reappeared to conduct himself with the utmost decorum. He did not even fidget when referred to pointedly as 'the other young man' by Mrs. Watson, with an accompaniment of nods and blinks and wreathed smiles which was, to say the least, suggestive. Geoff's manners could be trusted under all circumstances, and the little meal passed off charmingly.

'Good-bye,' said Mrs. Watson, after she was safely seated in the carriage, as Clover sedulously tucked her wraps about her. 'It's really been a treat to see you. We shall talk of it often, and I know Ellen will say—Oh, thank you, Miss Carr, you always were the kindest—Yes, I know it isn't Miss Carr, and I ought to remember, but somehow—Good-bye, Mrs. Page. Somehow—it's very pretty up here certainly, and you have every comfort I'm sure, and you seem—But it will be getting dark before long, and I don't like the idea of leaving you young things up here by yourselves. Don't you ever feel a little afraid in the evenings? I suppose there are not any wild animals— though I remember—But there, I mustn't say anything to discourage you, since you are here, and have got to stay.'

'Yes, we have to stay,' said Clover, as she shook hands with Mr. Phillips, 'and happily it is just what we all like best to do.' She watched the carriage for a moment or two as it bumped down the road, its brake grinding sharply against the wheels; then she turned to the others with a look of comically real relief.

'It seems like a bad dream! I had forgotten how Phil and I used to feel when Mrs. Watson went on like that, and she always did go on like that. How did we stand her?'

'Ellen seems nice,' remarked Elsie, 'poor Ellen!'

'Geoff,' added Clarence, vindictively, 'this must not happen again. You and I must go to work below and shave off the hill and make it twice as steep! It will never do to have the High Valley made easy of access to old ladies from Boston who— —'

'Who call you "the other young man",' put in naughty Elsie. 'Never mind, Clare. I share your feelings, but I don't think there is any risk. There is only one of her, and I am quite certain, from the scared look with which she alluded to our "wild beasts", that she never proposes to come again.'

CHAPTER SEVEN : THORNS AND ROSES

'Geoff,' said Clover as they sat at dinner two days later, 'couldn't we start early when we go in tomorrow to meet Rose, and have the morning at St. Helen's? There are quite a lot of little errands to be done, and it's a long time since we saw Poppy or the Hopes.'

'Just as early as you like,' replied her husband. 'It's a free day, and I am quite at your service.'

So they breakfasted at a quarter before six, and by a quarter past were on their way to St. Helen's, passing, as Clover remarked, through three zones of temperature; for it was crisply cold when they set out, temperately cool at the lower end of the Ute Pass, and blazing hot on the sandy plain.

'We certainly do get a lot of climate for our money out here,' observed Geoff.

They reached the town a little before ten, and went first of all to see Mrs. Marsh, for whom Clover had brought a basket of fresh eggs. She never entered the house without being sharply carried back to former days, and made .to feel that the intervening time was dreamy and unreal, so absolutely unchanged was it. There was the rickety piazza on which she and Phil had so often sat, the bare, unhomelike parlour, the rocking-chairs swinging all at once, timed as it were to an accompaniment of coughs; but the occupants were not the same. Many sets of invalids had succeeded each other at Mrs. Marsh's since those old days; still the general effect was precisely similar.

Mrs. Marsh, who only was unchanged, gave them a warm welcome. Grateful little Clover never had forgotten the many kindnesses shown •to her and Phil, and requited them in every way that was in her power. More than once when Mrs. Marsh was poorly or overtired, she had carried her off to the High Valley for a rest; and she never failed to pay her a visit whenever she spent a day at St. Helen's.

Their next call was at the Hopes'. They found Mrs. Hope darning stockings on the back piazza which commanded a view of the mountain range. She always claimed the entire credit of Clover's match, declaring that if she had not matronized her out to the Valley and introduced her and Geoff to each other, they would never have met. Her droll airs of proprietorship over their happiness were infinitely amusing to Clover.

'I think we should have got at each other somehow, even if you had not been in existence,' she told her friend; 'marriages are made in Heaven, as we all know. Nobody could have prevented ours.'

'My dear, that is just where you are mistaken. Nothing is easier than to prevent marriages. A mere straw will do it. Look at the countless old maids all over the world; and probably nearly every one of them came within half an inch of perfect happiness, and just missed it. No, depend on it, there is nothing like a wise, judicious, discriminating friend at such junctures to help matters along. You may thank me that Geoff isn't at this moment wedded to some stiff-necked British maiden, and you eating your head off in single-blessedness at Burnet.'

'Rubbish!' said Clover. 'Neither of us is capable of it;' but Mrs. Hope stuck to her convictions. She was delighted to see them, as she always was, and no less the bottle of beautiful cream, the basket full of fresh lettuces, and the bunch of Mariposa lilies which they had brought. Clover never went into St. Helen's empty-handed.

Here they took luncheon No. 1—consisting of sponge-cake and claret-cup, partaken of while gazing across at Cheyenne Mountain, which was at one of its most beautiful moments, all aerial blue streaked with sharp sunshine at the summit. It was the one defect of the High Valley, Clover thought, that it gave no glimpse of Cheyenne.

Luncheon No. 2 came a little later, with Marian Chase, whom everyone still called 'Poppy' from preference and long habit. She was perfectly well now, but she and her family had grown so fond of

St. Helen's that there was no longer any talk of their going back to the East. She had just had some beautiful California plums sent her by an admirer, and insisted on Clover's eating them with an accompaniment of biscuits and 'natural soda water'.

'I want you and Alice Perham to come out next week for two nights,' said Clover, while engaged in this agreeable occupation. 'My friend Mrs. Browne arrives today, and she is by far the greatest treat we have ever had to offer to anyone since we lived in the Valley. You will delight in her, I know. Could you come on Monday in the stage to the Ute Hotel, if we sent the carry-all over to meet you?'

'Why, of course. I never have any engagements when a chance comes for going to the dear Valley; and Alice has none, I am pretty sure. It will be perfectly delightful! Clover, you are an angel—"the Angel of the Pentstemon" I mean to call you,' glancing at the great sheaf of purple and white flowers which Clover had brought. 'It's a very good name. As for Elsie, she is "Our Lady of Raspberries"; I never saw such beauties as she fetched in week before last.'

Some very multifarious shopping for the two households followed, and by that time it was two o'clock and they were quite ready for luncheon No. 3—soup and sandwiches, procured at a restaurant. They were just coming away when an open carriage passed them, silk-lined, with a crest on the panel, jingling curb-chains, and silver-plated harnesses, all after the latest modem fashion, and drawn by a pair of fine grey horses. Inside was a young man, who returned with a stiff bow to Clover's salutation, and a gorgeously gowned young lady with rather a handsome face.

'Mr. and Mrs. Thurber Wade, I declare,' observed Geoffrey. 'I heard that they were expected.'

'Yes, Mrs. Wade is so pleased to have them come for the summer. We must go and call some day, Geoff, when I happen to have on my best bonnet. Do you think we ought to ask them out to the Valley?'

'That's just as you please. I don't mind if he doesn't. What fine horses! Aren't you conscious of a little qualm of regret, Clover?'

'What for? I don't know what you mean. Don't be absurd,' was all the reply he received, or in fact deserved.

And now it was time to go to the train. The minutes seemed long while they waited, but presently came the well-known shriek and rumble, and there was Rose herself, dimpled and smiling at the window, looking not a whit older than on the day of Katy's wedding seven years before. There was little Rose too, but she was by no means so unchanged as her mother, and certainly no longer little, surprisingly tall on the contrary, with her golden hair grown brown and braided in a pigtail, actually a pigtail.

She had the same bloom and serenity, however, and the same sedate, investigating look in her eyes. There was Mr. Browne too, but he was a brief joy, for there was only time to shake hands and exchange dates and promises of return, before the train started and bore him away toward Pueblo.

'Now,' said Rose, who seemed quite un-quenched by her three days of travel, 'don't let's utter one word till we are in the carriage, and then don't let's stop one moment for two weeks.'

'In the first place,' she began, as the carry-all mounting the hill, turned into Monument Avenue, where numbers of new houses had been built of late years, Queen Anne cottages in brick and stone, timber, and concrete, with here and there a more ambitious 'villa' of pink granite, all surrounded with lawns and roseries and vine-hung verandas and tinkling fountains. 'In the first place I wish to learn where all these people and houses come from. I was told that you lived in a lodge in the wilderness, but though I see plenty of lodges the wilderness seems wanting. Is this really an infant settlement?'

'It really is. That is, it hasn't come of age yet, being not quite twenty-one years old. Oh, you've no notion about our Western towns, Rose.

They're born and grown up all in a minute, like Hercules strangling the snakes in his cradle. I don't at all wonder that you are surprised.'

' "Surprised" doesn't express it. "Flabbergasted", though low, comes nearer my meaning. I have been breathless ever since we left Albany. First there was that enormous Chicago which knocked me all of a heap, then Denver, and now this! Never did I see such flowers and such coloured rocks, and never did anyone breathe such air. It sweeps all the dust and fatigue out of one in a minute. Boston seems quite small and dull in comparison, doesn't it, Roslein?'

'It isn't so big, but I love it the most,' replied that small person from the front seat, where she sat soberly taking all things in. 'Mamma, Uncle Geoff says I may drive when we get to the foot of a long hill we are just coming to. You won't be afraid, will you?'

'N-o; not if Uncle Geoff will keep his eye on the reins and stand ready to seize them if the horses begin to run. Rose just expresses my feelings,' she continued; 'but this is as beautiful as it is big. What is the name of that enchanting mountain over there—Cheyenne? Why, yes— that is the one that you used to write about in your letters when you first came out, I remember. It never made much impression on me— mountains never seem high in letters, somehow, but now I don't wonder. It's the loveliest thing I ever saw.'

Clover was much pleased at Rose's appreciation of her favourite mountain, and also with the intelligent way in which she noted everything they passed. Her eyes were as quick as her tongue; chattering all the time, she yet missed nothing of interest. The poppy-strewn plain, the green levels of the mesa delighted her; so did the wide stretches of blue distance, and she screamed with joy at the orange and red pinnacles in Odin's Garden.

'It is a land of wonders,' she declared. 'When I think how all my life I have been content to amble across the

Common, and down Winter Street to Hovey's, and now and then by way of adventure take the car to the Back Bay, and that I felt all the

90

while as if I were getting the cream and pick of everything, I am astonished at my own stupidity. Rose, are you not glad I did not let you catch whooping cough from Margaret Lyon? You were bent on doing it, you remember. If I had given you your way we should not be here now.'

Rose only smiled in reply. She was used to her little mother's vagaries and treated them in general with an indulgent attention.

The sun was quite gone from the ravines, but still lingered on the snow-powdered peaks above, when the carriage climbed the last steep zigzag and drew up before the 'Hut', whose upper windows glinted with the waning light. Rose looked about her and drew a long breath of surprise and pleasure.

'It isn't a bit like what I thought it would be,' she said; 'but it's heaps more beautiful. I simply put it at the head of all the places I ever saw.' Then Elsie came running on to the porch, and Rose jumped out into her arms.

'I thank the goodness and the grace That on my birth has smiled, And brought me to this blessed place, A happy Boston child!' she cried, hugging Elsie rapturously. 'You dear thing! How well you look! And how perfect it all is up here! And this is Mr. Page, whom I have known all about ever since the Hillsover days! And this is dear little Geoff! Clover, his eyes are exactly like yours! And where is your baby, Elsie?'

'Little wretch! She would go to sleep. I told her you were coming, and I did all I could, short of pinching, to keep her awake, sang, and repeated verses, and danced her up and down, but it was all of no use. She would put her knuckles in her eyes, and whimper and fret, and at last I had to give in. Babies are perfectly unmanageable when they are sleepy.'

'Most of us are. It's just as well. I can't half take it in as it is. It is much better to keep something for tomorrow. The drive was perfect, and the Valley is twice as beautiful as I expected it to be. And now I want to go into the house.'

Elsie had devoted her day to setting forth the Hut to advantage. She and Roxy had been to the very top of the East Canyon for flowers, and returned loaded with spoil. Bunches of coreopsis and vermilion-tipped painter's-brush adorned the chimney-piece; tall spikes of yucca rose from an Indian jar in one corner of the room, and a splendid sheaf of yellow columbines from another; fresh kinnikinnick was looped and wreathed about the pictures; and on the dining-table stood, most beautiful and fragile of all, a bowlful of Mariposa lilies, their delicate, lilac-streaked bells poised on stems so slender that the fairy shapes seemed to float in air, supported at their own sweet will. There were roses, too, and fragrant little knots of heliotrope and mignonette. With these Rose was familiar; the wild flowers were all new to her.

She ran from vase to vase in a rapture. They could scarcely get her upstairs to take off her things. Such a bright evening followed! Clover declared that she had not laughed so much in all the seven years since they parted. Rose seemed to fit at once and perfectly into the life of the place, while at the same time she brought the breath of her own more varied and different life to freshen and widen it. They all agreed that they had never had a visitor who gave so much and enjoyed so much. She and Geoffrey made friends at once, greatly to Clover's delight, and Clarence took to her in a manner astonishing to his wife, for he was apt to eschew strangers, and escape them when he could.

They all woke in the morning to a sense of holiday.

'Boys,' said Elsie at breakfast, 'this isn't at all a common, everyday day, and I don't want to do everyday things in it. I want something new and unusual to happen. Can't you abjure those wretched beasts of yours for once, and come with us to that sweet little canyon at the far end of the Ute, where we went the summer after I was married? We want to show it to Rose, and the weather is simply perfect.'

'Yes, if you'll give us half an hour or so to ride up and speak to Manuel.'

'All right. It will take at least as long as that to get ready.'

So Choo Loo hastily broiled chickens and filled bottles with coffee and cream; and by half past nine they were off, children and all, some on horseback, and some in the carry-all with the baskets, to Elsie's 'sweet little canyon', over which Pike's Peak rose in a lonely majesty like a sentinel at an outpost, and where flowers grew so thickly that, as Rose wrote to her husband, 'it was harder to find the in-betweens than the blossoms.' They came back, tired, hungry, and happy, just at nightfall; so it was not till the second day that Rose met the Youngs, about whom her curiosity was considerably excited. It seemed so odd, she said, to have 'only neighbours' and it made them of so much consequence.

They had been asked to dinner to meet Rose, which was a very formal and festive invitation for the High Valley, though the dinner must perforce be much as usual, and the party was inevitably the same. Imogen felt that it was an occasion, and wishing to do credit to it, she unpacked a gown which had not seen the light before since her arrival, and which had done duty as a dinner dress for two or three years at Bideford. It was of light blue mousseline-de-laine, made with a 'half-high top' and elbow sleeves, and trimmed with lace. A necklace of round coral beads adorned her throat, and a comb of the same material in her hair, which was done up in a series of wonderful loops filleted with narrow blue ribbons. She carried a pink fan. Lionel, who liked bright colours, was charmed at the effect; and altogether she set out in good spirits for the walk down the Pass, though she was prepared to be afraid of Rose, of whose brilliancy she had heard a little too much to make the idea of meeting her quite comfortable.

The party had just gathered in the sitting-room as they entered. Clover and Elsie were in pretty cotton dresses, as usual, and Rose, following their lead, had put on what at home she would have considered a morning gown, of linen lawn, white, with tiny bunches of forget-me-nots scattered over it, and a jabot of lace and blue ribbon. These toilettes seemed unduly simple to Imogen, who said within herself, complacently, 'There is one thing the Americans don't seem to understand, and that is the difference between common dressing and a regular dinner dress', preening herself the while in the blue mousseline-de-laine, and quite unconscious that Rose was inwardly remarking, 'My! Where did she get that gown? I never saw anything like it. It must have been made for Mrs. Noah, some years before the ark. And her hair! Just the ark style, too, and calculated to frighten the animals into good behaviour and obedience during the bad weather. Well, I put it at the head of all the extraordinary things I ever saw.'

It is just as well, on the whole, that people are not able to read each other's thoughts in society.

'You've only just come to America, I hear,' said Rose, taking a chair near Imogen. 'Do you begin to feel at home yet?'

'Oh, pretty well for that. I don't fancy that one ever gets to be quite at home anywhere out of their own country. It's very different over here from England, of course.'

'Yes, but some parts of America are more different than some other parts. You haven't seen much of us as yet.'

'No, but all the parts I have seen seemed very much alike.'

'The High Valley and New York, for example.'

'Oh, I wasn't thinking of New York. I mean the plains and mountains and the Western towns. We didn't stop at any of them, of course; but seen from the railway they all look pretty much the same—wooden houses, you know, and all that.'

'What astonished us most was the distance,' said Rose. 'Of course we all learned from our maps, when we were at school, just how far it is across the continent; but I never realized it in the least till I saw it. It seemed so wonderful to go on day after day and never get to the end'

'Only about half-way to the end,' put in Clover. 'That question of distance is a great surprise; and if it perplexes you, Rose, it isn't wonderful that it should perplex foreigners. Do you recollect that Englishman, Gooff, whom we met at the table d'hote at Llanberis, when we were in Wales, and who accounted for the Charleston earthquake by saying that he supposed it had something to do with these hot springs close by.'

'What hot springs did he mean?'

'I am sure you would never guess unless I told you. The hot springs in the Yellowstone Park, to be sure—simply those, and nothing more! And when I explained that Charleston and the Yellowstone were about as distant from each other as Siberia and the place we were in, he only stared and remarked, "Oh, I think you must be mistaken".'

'And are they so far apart, then?' asked Imogen, innocently. 'Oh, Moggy, Moggy! What were your geography teachers thinking about?' cried her brother. 'It seems sometimes as if America were entirely left out of the maps used in English schools.'

'Lionel,' said his sister, 'how can you say such things? It isn't so at all; but of course we learned more about the important countries.' Imogen spoke quite artlessly; she had no intention of being rude.

'Great Scott!' muttered Clarence under his breath, while Rose flashed a look at Clover.

'Of course,' she said, sweetly, 'Burmah and Afghanistan and New Zealand and the Congo States would naturally interest you more— large heathen populations to Christianize and exterminate. There is nothing like fire and sword to establish a bond.'

'Oh, I didn't mean that. Of course, America is much larger than those countries.'

' "Plenty of us such as we are," ' quoted the wicked Rose.

'And pretty good what there is of us,' added Clover, glad of the appearance of dinner just then to create a diversion.

'That's quite a dreadful little person,' remarked Rose, as they stood at the doorway two hours later, watching the guests walk up the trail under the light of a glorious full moon. 'Her mind is just one inch across. You keep falling off the edge and hurting yourself. It's sad that she should be your only neighbour. I don't seem to like her a bit, and I predict that you will yet have some dreadful sort of a row with her, Clovy.'

'Indeed we shall not; nothing of the kind. She's really a good little thing at bottom; this angularity and stiffness that you object to is chiefly manner. Wait till she has been here long enough to learn the ways and wake up, and you will like her.'

'I'll wait,' said Rose, dryly. 'How much time should you say would be necessary, Clover? A hundred years? I should think it would take at least as long as that.'

'Lionel's a dear fellow. We are all very fond of him.'

'I can understand your being fond of him easily enough. Imogen! What a name for just that kind of girl. "Image" it ought to be. What' a figure of fun she was in that awful blue gown!'

The two weeks of Rose's visit sped only too rapidly. There was so much that they wanted to show her, and there were so many people whom they wanted her to see, and so many people who, as soon as they saw her, became urgent that she should do this and that with them, that life soon became a tangle of impossibilities. Rose was one of those charmers that cannot be hid. She had been a belle all her days, and she would be so till she died of old age, as Elsie told her.

Her friends of the High Valley gloried in her success; but all the time they had a private longing to keep her more to themselves, as one retires with two or three to enjoy a choice dainty of which there is not enough to go round in a larger company. They took her to the Cheyenne Canyons and the top of Pike's Peak; they carried her over the Marshall Pass and to many smaller places less known to fame, but no less charming in their way. Invitations poured in from St. Helen's, to lunch, to dinner, to afternoon teas; but of these Rose would accept none. She could lunch and dine in Boston, she declared, but she might never come to Colorado again, and what she thirsted for was canyons, and not less than one a day would content her insatiable appetite for them.

But though she would not go to St. Helen's, St. Helen's in a measure came to her. Marian Chase and Alice made their promised visit; Dr. and Mrs. Hope came out more than once, and Phil continually; while smart Bostonians whom Clover had never heard of turned up at Canyon Creek and the Ute Valley and drove over to call, having heard that Mrs. Deniston Browne was staying there. The High Valley became used to the roll of wheels and the tramp of horses' feet, and for the moment seemed a sociable, accessible sort of place to which it was a matter of course that people should repair. It was oddly different from the customary order of things, but the change was enlivening, and everybody enjoyed it with one exception.

This exception was Imogen Young. She was urged to join some of the excursions made by her friends below, but on one excuse or another she refused. She felt shy and left out where all the rest were so well-acquainted and so thoroughly at ease, and preferred to remain at home; but all the same, to have the others so gay and busy gave her a sense of loneliness and separation which was painful to bear. Clover tried more than once to persuade her out of her solitary mood; but she was too much occupied herself and too absorbed to take much time for coaxing a reluctant guest, and the others dispensed with her company quite easily; in fact, they were too busy to notice her absence much or ask questions. So the fortnight, which passed so quickly and brilliantly at the Hut, and was always afterward alluded to as 'that delightful time when Rose was here,' was anything but delightful at the 'Hutlet', where poor Imogen sat homesick and forlorn, feeling left alone on one side of all the pleasant things, scarcely realizing that it was her own choice and doing, and wishing herself back in Devonshire.

'Lion seems quite taken up with these new people and that Mrs. Browne,' she reflected. 'He's always going off with them to one place or another. I might as well be back in Bideford for all the use I am to him.' This was unjust, for Lionel was too anxious and worried over his sister's depressed looks and indisposition to share in the pleasures that were going on; but Imogen just then saw things through a gloomy medium, and not quite as they were. She felt dull and heavy-hearted, and did not seem able to rouse herself from her lassitude and weariness.

Out of the whole party no one was so perfectly pleased with her surroundings as the smaller Rose. Everything seemed to suit the little maid exactly. She made a delightful playfellow for the babies, telling them fairy stories by the dozen, and teaching them new games, and washing and dressing Phillida with all the gravity and decorum of an old nurse. They followed her about like two little dogs, and never left her side for a moment if they could possibly help it. All was fish that came to her happy little net, whether it was playing with little Geoff, going on excursions with the elders, scrambling up the steep side-canyons under Phil's escort in search of flowers and curiosities, or riding sober old Marigold to the Upper Valley as she was sometimes allowed to do. The only cloud in her perfect satisfaction was that she must some day go away.

'It won't be very pleasant when I get back to Boston, and don't have anything to do but just walk down Pinckney Street with Mary Anne to school, and slide a little bit on the Common when the snow comes and there aren't any big boys about, will it, Mamma?' she said, disconsolately.

'I shan't feel as if that were a great deal, I think.'

'I am afraid the High Valley is a poor preparation for West Cedar Street,' laughed Rose. 'It will seem a limited career to both of us at first. But cheer up, Poppet; I'm going to put you into a dancing-class this winter, and very likely at Christmas-time Papa will treat us both to a Moral Drayma. There are consolations, even in Boston.'

'That "even in Boston" is the greatest compliment the High Valley ever received,' said Clover, who happened to be within hearing. 'Such a moment will never come to it again.'

And now the last day came, as last days will. Mr. Browne returned from Mexico, with forty-eight hours to spare for enjoyment, which interval they employed in showing him the two things that Rose loved most—namely, the High Valley from top to bottom, and the North Cheyenne Canyon. The last luncheon was taken at Mrs. Hope's, who had collected a few choice spirits in honour of the occasion, and then they all took the Roses to the train, and sent them off loaded with fruit and flowers.

'Miss Young was extraordinarily queer and dismal last night,' said Rose to Clover as they stood a little aside from the rest on the platform. 'I can't quite see what ails her. She looks thinner than when we came, and doesn't seem to know how to smile; depend upon it she's going to be ill, or something. I wish you had a pleasanter neighbour—especially as she's likely to be the only one for some time to come.'

'Poor thing. I've neglected her of late,' replied Clover, penitently. 'I must make up for it now that you are going away. Really, I couldn't take my time for her while you were here, Rosy.'

'And I certainly couldn't let you. I should have resented it highly if you had. Oh dear, there's that whistle. We really have got to go. I hoped to the last that something might happen to keep us another day. Oh dear Clover—I wish we lived nearer each other. This country of ours is a great deal too wide.'

'Geoff,' said Clover, as they slowly climbed the hill, 'I never felt before that the High Valley was too far away

from people, but somehow I do tonight. It is quite terrible to have Rose go, and to feel that I may not see her again for years.'

'Did you want to go with her?'

'And leave you? No, dearest. But I am quite sure that there are no distances in Heaven, and when we get there we shall find that we all are to live next door to each other. It will be part of the happiness.'

'Perhaps so. Meanwhile I am thankful that my happiness lives close to me now. I don't have to wait till Heaven for that, which is the reason perhaps that for some years past Earth has seemed so very satisfactory to me.'

'Geoff, what an uncommonly nice way you have of putting things,' said Clover, nestling her head comfortably on his arm. 'On the whole I don't think the High Valley is so very far away.'

CHAPTER EIGHT : UNCONDITIONAL SURRENDER

'Have you seen Imogen Young today?' was Clover's first question on getting home.

'No. Lionel was in for a moment at noon, and said she was preserving raspberries; so, as I had a good deal to do, I did not go up. Why?'

'Oh, nothing in particular. I only wanted to know. Well, here we are, left to ourselves with not a Rose to our name. How we shall miss them! There's a letter from Johnnie for you by way of consolation.'

But the letter did not prove in the least consoling, for it was to break to them a piece of disappointing news.

'The Daytons have given up their Western trip,' wrote Johnnie. 'Mrs. Dayton's father is very ill at Elberon; she has gone to him, and there is almost no chance of their getting away all this summer. It really is a dreadful disappointment, for we had set our hearts on our visit, and Papa had made all his arrangements to be absent for six weeks— which you know is a thing not easily done, or undone. Then Debby and Richard had been promised a holiday, and Dorry was going in a yacht with some friends to the Thousand Islands. It all seemed so nicely settled, and here comes this blow to unsettle it. Well, Dieu dispose—there is nothing for it but resignation, and unpacking our hopes and ideas and putting them back again in their usual shelves and corners. We must make what we can of the situation, and of course, it isn't anything so very hard to have to pass the summer in Burnet with Papa; still I was that wild with disappointment at the first, that I actually went the length of suggesting that we should go all the same, and pay our own travelling expenses! You can judge from this how desperate my state of mind must have been. Papa, as you may naturally suppose, promptly vetoed the proposal as impossible, and no doubt he was right. I am growing gradually resigned to Fate now, but all the same I cannot yet think of the blessed Valley and all of you, and—and the happy time we are not going to have, without feeling quite like "weeping a little weep". How I wish that we possessed a superfluous income!'

'Now,' said Elsie, and her voice too sounded as if a 'little weep' were not far off, 'isn't that too bad? No Papa this year, and no Johnnie. I suppose we are spoiled, but the fact is, I have grown to count on the Daytons and their car as confidently as though they were the early and the latter rain.' Her arch little face looked quite long and disconsolate.

'So have I,' said Clover. 'It doesn't bear talking about, does it?'

She had been conscious of late of a great longing after her father. She had counted confidently on his visit, and the sense of disappointment was bitter. She put away her bonnet: and folded her gloves with a very sober face. A sort of disenchantment seemed to have fallen on the Valley since the coming of this bad news and the departure of Rose.

'This will never do,' she told herself at last, after standing some moments at the window looking across at the peak through a blur of tears. 'I must brace up and comfort Elsie.'

But Elsie was not to be comforted all at once, and the wheels of that evening drove rather heavily.

Next morning, as soon as her usual tasks were despatched, Clover ordered Marigold saddled and started for the Youngs'. Rose's last remarks had made her uneasy about Imogen, and she remembered with compunction how little she had seen of her for a fortnight past.

No one but Sholto, Lionel's great deer-hound, came out to meet her as she dismounted at the door. His bark of welcome brought Ah Lee from the back of the house.

'Missee not velly well, me thinkee,' he observed.

'Is Missy ill? Where is Mr. Young, then?'

'He go two hours ago to Uppey Valley. Missee not sick then.'

'Is she in her room?' asked Clover. 'Tie Marigold in the shade, please, and I will go in and see her.'

'All litee.'

The bedroom door was closed, and Clover tapped twice before she heard a languid 'Come in'. Imogen was lying on the bed in her morning dress, with flushed cheeks and tumbled hair. She looked at Clover with a sort of perplexed surprise.

'My poor child, what is the matter? Have you a bad headache?'

'Yes, I think so, rather bad. I kept up till Lion had had his breakfast, and then everything seemed to go round, and I had to come and lie down. So stupid of me!' impatiently; 'but I thought perhaps it would pass off after a little.'

'And has it?' asked Clover, pulling off her gloves and taking Imogen's hand. It was chilly rather than hot, but the pulse seemed weak and quick. Clover began to feel anxious, but did her best to hide it under a cheerful demeanour lest she should startle Imogen. 'Were you quite well yesterday?' she asked.

'Yes—that is, I wasn't ill. I had no headache then, but I think I haven't been quite right for some time back, and I tried to do some raspberries and felt very tired. I dare say it's only getting acclimated. I'm really very strong. Nothing ever was the matter with me at home.'

'Now,' said Clover brightly, 'I'll tell you what you are going to do; and that is to put on your wrapper, make yourself comfortable, and take a long sleep. I have come to spend the day, and I will give Lion his luncheon and see to everything if only you will lie still. A good rest would make you feel better, I am sure.'

'Perhaps so,' said Imogen, doubtfully. She was too miserable to object, and with a docility foreign to her character submitted to be undressed, to have her hair brushed and knotted up, and a bandage of cold water and eau de cologne laid on her forehead. This passive compliance was so unlike her that Clover felt her anxieties increase. 'Matters must be serious,' she reflected, 'when Imogen Young agrees meekly to any proposal from anybody.'

She settled her comfortably, shook up the pillows, darkened the window, threw a light shawl over her, and sat beside the bed fanning gently till Imogen fell into a troubled sleep. Then she stole softly away and busied herself in washing the breakfast things and putting the rooms to rights. The young mistress of the house had evidently felt unequal to her usual tasks, and everything was left standing just as it was.

Clover was recalled by a cry from the bedroom, and hurried back to find Imogen sitting up, looking confused and startled.

'What is it? Is anything the matter?' Imogen demanded. Then, before Clover could reply, she came to herself and understood.

'Oh, it is you,' she said. 'What a comfort! I thought you were gone away.'

'No, indeed, I have no idea of going away. I was just in the other room, straightening things out a little. It was settled that I was to stay to lunch and keep Lionel company, you remember.'

'Ah, yes. It is very good of you, but I'm afraid there isn't much for luncheon,' sinking back on her pillows again. 'Ah Lee will know. I don't seem able to think clearly of anything.'

She sighed, and presently was asleep again, or seemed to be so, and Clover went back to her work.

So it went all day—broken slumbers, confused wakings, increasing fever, and occasional moments of bewilderment. Clover was sure that it was a serious illness, and sent Lionel down with a note to say that either Geoff or Clarence must go in at once and bring out Dr. Hope, that she herself was a fixture at the other house for the night at least, and would like a number of things sent up, of which she enclosed a list. This note threw the family into a wild dismay. Life in the High Valley was only meant for well people, as Elsie had once admitted. Illness at once made the disadvantage of so lonely and inaccessible a place apparent—with the doctor sixteen miles distant, and no medicines or other appliances of a sick-room to be had short of St. Helen's.

Dr. Hope reached them late in the evening. He pronounced that Imogen had an attack of 'mountain fever', a milder sort of typhoid not uncommon in the higher elevations of Colorado. He hoped it would be a light case, gave full directions, and promised to send out medicines and to come again in three days. Then he departed, and Clover, as she watched him ride down the trail, felt as a shipwrecked mariner might, left alone on a desert island—astray and helpless, and quite at a loss as to what first to do.

There were too many things to be done, however, to allow of her long indulging this feeling, and presently her wits cleared and she was able to confront the task before her with accustomed sense and steadiness. Imogen could not be left alone, that was evident; and it was evident that she herself was the person who must stay with her.

Elsie could not be spared from her baby, and Geoffrey, beside being more especially interested in the Youngs, would be far more amenable and less refractory than Clarence at a curtailment of his domestic privileges. So, pluckily and reasonably, she 'buckled to' the work so plainly set for her, established herself and her belongings in the spare chamber, gathered the reins of the household and the sick-room into her hands, and began upon what she knew might prove to be a long, hard bout of patience and vigilance, resolved to do her best each day as it came and let the next day take care of itself, minding nothing, no fatigue or homesickness or difficulty, if only Imogen could be properly cared for and get well.

After the first day or two matters fell into regular grooves. The attack proved a light one, as the doctor had hoped. Imogen was never actually in danger, but there was a good deal of weakness and depression, occasional wandering of mind, and always the low, underlying fever, not easily detected save by the clinical thermometer. In her semi-delirious moments she would ramble about Bideford and the people there, or hold Clover's hand tight, calling her 'Isabel', and imploring her not to like 'Mrs. Geoff' better than she liked her. It was the first glimpse that Clover had ever caught of this unhappy tinge of jealousy in Imogen's mind; it grieved her, but it also explained some things that had been perplexing, and she grew very pitiful and tender over the poor girl, away from home among strangers, and so ill and desolate.

The most curious thing about it all was the extraordinary preference which the patient showed for Clover above all her other nurses. If Euphane came to sit beside her, or Elsie, or even Lionel, while Clover took a rest, Imogen was manifestly uneasy and unhappy. She never said that she missed Clover, but lay watching the door with a strained, expectant look which melted into relief as soon as Clover appeared. Then she would feebly move her fingers to lay hold of Clover's hand, and holding it fast, would fall asleep satisfied and content. It seemed as if the sense of comfort which Clover's appearance that first morning had given continued when she was not quite herself, and influenced her.

'It's queer how much better she likes you than any of the rest of us,' Lionel said one day. Clover felt oddly pleased at this remark. It was a new experience to be preferred by Imogen Young, and she could not but be gratified.

'Though very likely,' she told herself, 'she will stiffen up again when she gets well; so I must be prepared for it, and not mind when it happens.'

Meanwhile Imogen could not have been better cared for anywhere than she was in the High Valley. Clover had a natural aptitude for nursing. She knew by instinct what a sick person would like and dislike, what would refresh and what weary, what must be remembered and what avoided. Her inventive faculties also came into full play under the pressure of the little daily emergencies, when exactly the thing wanted was sure not to be at hand. It was quite wonderful how she devised substitutes for all sorts of deficiencies. Elsie, amazed at her cleverness, declared herself sure that if Dr. Hope were to say that a roc's egg was needful for Imogen's recovery, Clover would reply, as a matter of course, 'Certainly—I will send it up directly,' and thereupon proceed to concoct one out of materials already in the house, which would answer as well as the original article and do Imogen just as much good. She cooked the nicest little sick-room messes, giving them variety by cunningly devised flavours, and she originated cooling drinks out of sago and arrowroot and tamarinds and fruit juices and ice, which Imogen would take when she refused everything else. Her lightness of touch and bright, equable calmness were unfailing. Dr. Hope said she would make the fortune of any ordinary hospital, and that she was so evidently cut out for a nurse that it seemed a clear subversion of the plans of Providence that she should ever have married—a speech for which the doctor got little thanks from anybody, for Clover declared that she hated hospitals and sick folks, and never wanted to nurse anybody but the people she loved best, and then only when she couldn't help herself; while Geoffrey treated the facetious physician to the blackest of frowns, and privately confided to Elsie that the doctor, good fellow that he was, deserved a kicking, and he shouldn't mind being the one to administer it.

By the end of a fortnight the fever was conquered, and then began the slow process of building up exhausted strength, and fanning the dim spark of life once again into a generous flame. This is apt to be the most trying part of an illness to those who nurse; the excitement of anxiety and danger being past, the space between convalescence and complete recovery seems very wide, and hard to bridge over. Clover found it so. Imogen's strength came back slowly; all her old vigour and decision seemed lost; she was listless and despondent, and needed to be coaxed and encouraged and cheered as much as does an ailing child.

She did not 'stiffen', however, as Clover had feared she might do; on the contrary, her dependence upon her favourite nurse seemed to increase, and on the days when she was most languid and hopeless she clung most to her. There was a wistful look in her eyes as they followed Clover in her comings and goings, and a new, tender tone in her voice when she spoke to her; but she said little, and after she was able to sit up she just lay back in her chair and gazed at the mountains in a dreamy fashion for hours together.

'This will never do,' Lionel declared. 'We must hearten her up somehow,' which he proceeded to do, after the blundering fashion of the ordinary man, by a series of thrilling anecdotes about cattle and their vagaries, refractory cows who turned upon their herders and 'horned' them, and wild steers who chased mounted men, overtook and gored them; how Felipe was stampeded and Pepe just escaped with his life. The result of this 'heartening' process was that Imogen, in her weak state, conceived a horror of ranch work, and passed the hours of his absence in a subdued agony of apprehension concerning him. He was very surprised and contrite when scolded by Clover.

'What shall I talk to her about, then?' he demanded ruefully. 'I can't bear to see her sit so dull and silent. Poor Moggy! And cattle are the only subjects of conversation that we have up here.'

'Talk about yourself and herself and the funny things that happened when you were little, and pet her all you can; but pray don't allude to horned animals of any kind. She's so quiet only because she is weak. Presently we shall see her brighten.'

And so they did. With the first breath of autumn, full of cool sparkle and exhilaration, Imogen began to rally.

Colour stole back to her lips, vigour to her movements; each day she could do a little and a little more. Her first coming out to dinner was treated as a grand event. She was placed in a cushioned chair and served like a queen. Lionel was in raptures at seeing her in her old place, at the head of the table, 'better than new', as he asserted; and certainly Imogen had never in her life been so pretty. They had cut her long hair during her illness because it was falling out so fast; the short rings round her face were very becoming, the sunburn of the summer had worn off and her complexion was delicately fair. Clover had dressed her in a loose jacket of pale-pink flannel which Elsie had fitted and made for her; it was trimmed with soft frills of lace, and knots of ribbon, and Geoff had brought up a half-opened tea rose which exactly matched it.

'I shall carry you home with me when I go,' Clover told Imogen as she helped her undress. 'You must come down and make us a good long visit. I can't and won't have you left alone up here, to keep the house and sit for hours every day imagining that Lionel is being gored by wild bulls.'

'When you go?' repeated Imogen, in a dismayed tone; 'but yes, of course you must go— what was I thinking of?'

'Not while you need me,' said Clover, soothingly. 'But you are nearly well now, and will soon be able to do everything for yourself.'

'I am absolutely silly,' said Imogen, with her eyes full of tears. 'What extraordinary things fevers are! I declare I am as bad as any child. It is absurd, but the mere idea of having to give you up makes me quite cold and miserable.'

'But you won't have to give me up; we are going to be neighbours still, and see each other every day. You are acclimated now, Dr. Hope says.'

'Yes—I hope so; I am sure I hope so. And yet, do you know, I almost think I would go through the fever all over again for the sake of having you take care of me!'

'Why, my dear child, what a thing to say! It's the greatest compliment I ever had in my life, but yet— —'

'It's no compliment at all. I should never think of paying you compliments. I couldn't.'

'That is sad for me. Compliments are nice things, I think.'

Imogen suddenly knelt down and put her arms on Clover's lap as she sat by the window.

'I want to tell you something,' she said in a broken voice. 'I was so unjust when I came over—so rude and unkind in my thoughts. You will hardly believe it, but I didn't like you!'

'I can believe it without any particular difficulty. Everybody can't like me, you know.'

'Everybody ought to. You are simply the best, dearest, truest person I ever knew. Oh, I can't half say what you are, but I know! You have heaped coals of fire on my head. Perhaps that's the reason my hair has fallen off so,' with a mirthless laugh. 'I used to feel them burn and burn, on those nights when I lay all scorching up with fever, and you sat beside me so cool and sweet and patient. And there is more still. I was jealous because I fancied that Isabel liked you better than she did me. Did you ever suspect that?'

'Never till you were ill. Some little things that you muttered when you were not quite yourself put the idea into my head.'

'I can't think why I was so idiotic about it. Of course she liked you best—who wouldn't? How horrid it was in me to feel so! I used to try hard not to, but it was of no use; I kept on all the same.'

'But you're not jealous now, I hope?'

'No, indeed,' shaking her head. 'The feeling seems all burnt out of me. If I am ever jealous again it will be just the other way, for fear you will care for her and not at all for me.'

'I do believe you are making me a declaration of attachment!' cried Clover, amazed beyond expression at this outburst, but inexpressibly pleased. The stiff, reserved Imogen seemed transformed. Her face glowed with emotion, her words came in a torrent. She was altogether different from her usual self.

'Attachment! If I were not attached to you I should be the most ungrateful wretch going. Here you have stayed away from home all these weeks, and worked like a servant making me all those lovely lemon-squashes and things, and letting your own affairs go to wrack and ruin, and you never seemed to remember that you had any affairs, or that there was such a thing as getting tired—never seemed to remember anything except to take care of me. You are an angel!— there is nobody like you. I don't believe anyone else in the world would have done what you did for a stranger who had no claim upon you.'

'That is absurd,' said Clover, frightened at the probable effect of all this excitement on her patient, and trying to treat the matter lightly. 'You exaggerate things dreadfully. We all have a claim on each other, especially here in the Valley where there are so few of us. If I had been ill you would have turned to and helped nurse me as I did you, I am sure.'

'I shouldn't have known how.'

'You would have learned how just as I did. Emergencies are wonderful teachers. Now, dear Imogen, you must get to bed. If you excite yourself like this you will have a bad night and be put back.'

'Oh, I'll sleep. I promise you that I will sleep if only you will let me say just one more thing. I won't go on any more about the things you have done, though it's all true—and I don't exaggerate in the least, for all that you say I do; but never mind that, only please tell me that you forgive me. I can't rest till you say that.'

'For what—for not liking me at first; for being jealous of Isabel? Both were natural enough, I think. Isabel was your dearest friend; and I was a newcomer, an interloper. I never meant to come between you, I am sure; but I dare say that I seemed to do so, and I can understand it all easily. There is no question of forgiving between us, dear, only of forgetting. We are friends now, and we will both love Isabel; and I will love you if you will let me, and you shall love me.'

'How good you are!' exclaimed Imogen, as Clover bent over for a good-night kiss. She put her arms round Clover's neck and held her tight for a moment.

'Yes, indeed,' she sighed. 'I don't deserve it after my bad behaviour, but I shall be only too glad if I may be your friend. I don't believe any other girl in the world has two so good as you and Isabel.'

'Don't lie awake to think over our perfections,' said Clover, as she withdrew with the candle. 'Go to sleep, and remember that you are coming down to the Hut with me for a visit, whenever I go.'

Dr. Hope, however, negatived this suggestion decidedly. He was an autocrat with his sick people, and no one dared dispute his decisions.

'What your young woman needs is to get away from the Valley for a while into lower air; and what you need is to have her go, and forget that you have been nursing her,' he told Clover. 'There is a look of tension about you both which is not the correct thing. She'll improve much faster at St. Helen's than here, and besides, I want her under my eye for a while. Mary shall send up an invitation tomorrow, and mind that you make her accept it.'

So the next day came the most cordial of notes from Mrs. Hope, asking Imogen to spend a fortnight with her. 'Dr. Hope wishes to consider you his patient a little longer,' she wrote, 'and says the lower level will do you good; and I want you as much as he does for other reasons. St. Helen's is rather empty just now, in this betwixt-and-between season, and a visitor will be a real godsend to me. I am so afraid that you will be disobliging, and say "No", that I have made the doctor put it in the form of a prescription; and please tell Clover that we count upon her to see that you begin to take the remedy without delay.'

And sure enough, on the doctor's prescription paper, with the regular appeal to Jupiter which heads all prescriptions, a formula was enclosed settling forth with due professional precision that Miss Imogen Young was to be put in a carry-all, 'well shaken' on the way down, and taken in fourteen daily doses in the town of St. Helen's. 'Immediate.'

'How very good of them!' said Imogen. 'Everybody is so wonderfully good to me! I think America must be the kindest country in the world!'

She made no difficulty about accepting the invitation, and resigned herself to the will of her friends with a docility that was astonishing to everybody except Clover, who was in the secret of her new-born resolves. They packed her things at once, and Lionel drove her down to St. Helen's the very day after the reception of Mrs. Hope's note.

Imogen parted from the sisters with a warm embrace, but she clung longest to Clover.

'You will let me come for a night or two when I return, before I settle again at home, won't you?' she said. 'I shall be half-starved to see you, and a mile is a goodish bit to get over when you're not strong.'

'Why, of course,' said Clover, delighted. 'We shall count on it, and Lion has promised to stay with us all the time you are away.'

'I do think that girl has experienced a change of heart,' remarked Elsie, as they turned to go indoors. 'She seems really fond of you, and almost fond of me. It is no wonder, I am sure, so far as you are concerned, after all you have done for her. I never supposed she could look so pretty or come so near being agreeable as she does now. Evidently mountain-fever is what the English emigrant of the higher classes needs to thaw him out and attune him to American ways.. It's a pity they can't all be inoculated with it on landing. Now, Clovy—my dear, sweet old Clovy —what fun it is to have you at home again!' she went on, giving her sister a rapturous embrace. 'I wouldn't mention it so long as you had to be away, but I have missed you horribly. "There's no luck about the house" when you are not in it. We have all been out of sorts—Geoff quite down in the mouth, little Geoff not at all contented with me as a mother; even Euphane has worn a long face and exhibited a tendency to revert to the Isle of Man, which she never showed so long as you were to the fore. As for me, I have felt like a person with one lung, or half a head—all broken up, and unlike myself. Oh, dear! How good it is to get you back, and be able to consult you and look at you! Come upstairs at once, and unpack your things, and we will play that you have never been away, and that the last month is nothing but a disagreeable dream from which we have waked up.'

'It is delightful to get back,' admitted Clover; 'still the month has had its nice side, too. Imogen is so sweet and grateful and demonstrative that it would astonish you. She is like a different girl. I really think she has grown to love me.'

'I should say that nothing was more probable. But don't let's talk of Imogen now. I want you all to myself.'

The day had an ending as happy as unexpected. This was the letter that Lionel Young brought back that evening from Johnnie at Burnet:

DEAREST SISTERS,

What do you think has happened? Something as enchanting as it is surprising! I wrote you about Dorry's having the grippe; but I would not tell you what a serious affair it was, because you were all so anxious and occupied about Miss Young that I did not like to add to your worries more than I could help. He was pretty ill for nearly a week; and though on the mend now, he is much weakened and run down, and Papa, I can see, considers him still in a poor way. There is no chance of his being able to go back to the works for a couple of months yet, and we were casting about as to the best way of giving him a change of air, when, last night, came a note from Mr. Dayton to say that he has to take a business run to Salt Lake, with a couple of his directors, and there are two places in car 47 at our service if any of us still care to make the trip to Colorado, late as it is. We had to answer at once, and we took only ten minutes to make up our minds. Dorry and I are to start for Chicago tomorrow, and will be with you on Thursday if all goes well—and for a good long visit, as the company have given Dorry a two months' vacation. We shall come back like common folks at our own charges, which is an unusual extravagance for the Carr family; but Papa says sickness is a valid reason for spending money, while mere pleasure isn't. He thinks the journey will be the very thing for Dorry. It has all come so suddenly that I am quite bewildered in my mind. I don't at all like going away and leaving Papa alone; but he is quite decided about it, and there is just the bare chance that Katy may run out for a week or two, so I am going to put my scruples in my pocket and take the good the gods provide, prepared to be very happy. How perfectly charming it will be to see you all! Somehow I never pined for you and the Valley so much as I have of late. It was really an awful blow when the August plan came to nothing, but Fate is making amends. Thursday! Only think of it! You will just have time to put towels in our rooms and fill the pitchers before we are there. I speak for the west corner one in the guest cabin, which I had last year. Our dear love to you all. Your affectionate JOHNNIE.

P.S. Please tell Mr. Young how happy we are that his sister is recovering.

'This is too delicious!' said Elsie, when she had finished reading this letter. 'Dorry, who never has been here, and John, and for October, when we so rarely have anybody! I think it is a sort of "reward of merit" for you, Clover, for taking such good care of Imogen Young.'

'It's a most delightful one if it is. I half wish now that we hadn't asked Lion to stay while his sister is gone. He's a dear good fellow, but it would be nicer to have the others quite to ourselves, don't you think so?'

'Clover dear,' said Elsie, looking very wise and significant, 'did it never occur to you that there might be a little something like a sentiment or tenderness between John and Lionel? Are you sure that she would be so thoroughly pleased if we sent him off and kept her to ourselves?'

'Certainly not. I never thought of such a thing.'

'You never do think of such things. I am much sharper about them that you are, and I have observed a tendency on the part of Miss John to send messages to that young man in her letters, and always in postscripts. Mark that, postscripts! There is something very suspicious in postscripts, and he invariably blushes immensely when I deliver them.'

'You are a great deal too sharp,' responded Clover, laughing. 'You see though millstones that don't exist. It would be very nice if it were so, but it isn't. I don't believe a word about your postcripts and blushes; you've imagined it all.' 'Some people are born stupid in these directions,' retorted Elsie. 'I'll bet you Phillida's back hair against the first tooth that Geoffy loses that I am right.'

CHAPTER NINE: THE EDCHOES IN THE EAST CANYON

Lionel certainly did redden when Johnnie's message was delivered to him. The quick-eyed Elsie noted it and darted a look at Clover, but Clover only shook her head slightly in return. Each sister adhered to her own opinion. They were very desirous that the High Valley should make a favourable impression on Dorry, for it was his first visit to them. The others had all been there except Katy, and she had seen Cheyenne and St. Helen's, but to Dorry everything west of the Mississippi was absolutely new. He was a very busy person in these days, and quite the success of the Carr family in a moneyed point of view. The turn for mechanics which he exhibited in boyhood had continued, and determined his career. Electrical science had attracted his attention in its earlier, half- developed stages; he had made a careful study of it, and qualified himself for the important position which he held under the company, which was fast revolutionizing the lighting and street-car system of Burnet, now growing to be a large manufacturing centre. This was doing well for a young fellow not quite twenty-five, and his family were very proud of him. He was too valuable to his employers to be easily spared, and except for the enforced leisure of the grippe it might probably have been years before he felt free to make his sisters in Colorado a visit, in which case nothing would have happened that did happen.

'Dear, steady old Sobersides!' said Elsie, as she spread a fresh cover over the shelf which did duty for a bureau in the Bachelors' Room; 'I wonder what he will think of it all. I'm afraid he will be scandalized at our scrambling ways, and our having no regular church, and consider us a set of half-heathen Bohemians.'

T don't believe it. Dorry has too much good sense, and has seen too much of the world among business men to be easily shocked. And our little Sunday service is very nice, I think; Geoff reads so reverently—and for sermons, we have our pick of the best there are.'

T know, and I like them dearly myself; but I seem to feel that Dorry will miss the pulpit and sitting in a regular pew. He's rather that sort of person, don't you think?'

'You are too much inclined to laugh at Dorry,' said Clover, reprovingly, 'and he doesn't deserve it of you. He's a thoroughly good, sensible fellow and has excellent abilities, Papa says—not brilliant, but very sound. I don't like to have you speak so of him.'

'Why Clovy, my little Clovy, I almost believe you are scolding me! Let me look at you—yes, there's quite a frown on your forehead, and your mouth has the firm look of Grandpapa Carr's daguerreotype. I'll be good— really I will. Don't fire again—I've "come down" like the coon in the anecdote. Dorry's a dear, and you are another, and I'm ever so glad he's coming; but really, it's not in human nature not to laugh at the one solemn person in a frivolous family like ours, now is it?'

'See that you behave yourself, then, and I'll not scold you any more,' replied Clover, magisterially, and ignoring the last question. She marred the effect of her lecture by kissing Elsie as she spoke; but it was hard to resist the temptation, Elsie was so droll and coaxing, and so very pretty.

They expected to find Dorry still something of an invalid, and made preparations accordingly but there was no sign of debility in his jump from the carriage or his run up the steps to greet them. He was a little thinner than usual, but otherwise seemed quite himself.

'It's the air,' explained Johnnie, 'this blessed Western air! He was forlorn when we left Burnet, and so tired when we got to Chicago; but after that he improved with every mile, and when we reached Denver this morning he seemed fresher than when we started. I do think Colorado air the true elixir of life.'

'It is quite true, what she says. I feel like a different man already,' added Dorry. 'Clover, you look a little pulled down yourself. Was it nursing Miss What's-her-name?'

'I'm all right. Another day or two will quite rest me. I came home only the day before yesterday, you see. How delicious it is to have you both here! Dorry dear, you must have some beef-tea directly — Euphane has a little basin of it ready — and dinner will be in about an hour.'

'Beef-tea! What for? I don't need anything of the sort, I assure you. Roast mutton, which I seem to smell in the distance, is much more in my line. I want to look about and see your house. What do you call that snow-peak over there? This is a beautiful place of yours, I declare.'

'Papa would open his eyes if he could see him,' remarked Johnnie, confidentially, when she got her sisters to herself a little later. 'It's like a miracle the way he has come up. He was so dragged and miserable, and so very cross only three days ago. Now, you dear things, let me look at you both. Are you quite well? How are the brothers-in-law? Where are the babies, and what have you done with Miss Young?'

'The brothers-in-law are all right. They will be back presently. There is a round-up today, which was the reason we sent Isadore in with the carriage; no one else could be spared. The babies are having their supper — you will see them anon — and Imogen has gone for a fortnight to St. Helen's.'

'Oh!' Johnnie turned aside and began to take down her hair. 'Mr. Young is with her, I suppose.'

'No, indeed, he is here, and staying with us. You will see him at dinner.'

'Oh!' said Johnnie again. There was a difference between these two 'ohs', which Elsie's quick ear detected.

'Please unlock that valise,' went on Johnnie, 'and take out the dress on top. This I have on is too dreadfully dusty to be endured.'

119

Joanna Carr had grown up very pretty; many people considered her the handsomest of the four sisters. Taller than any of them except Katy, and of quite a different build, large, vigorous, and finely formed, she had a very white skin, hair of pale bronze-brown, and beautiful velvety dark eyes with thick curling lashes. She had a turn for dress too, and all colours suited her. The woollen gown of cream-yellow which she now put on seemed exactly what was needed to throw up the tints of her hair and complexion; but she would look equally well on the morrow in blue. With quick accustomed fingers she whisked her pretty locks into a series of artlessly artful loops, with little blowing rings about the forehead, and stuck a bow in here and a pin there talking all the time, and finally caught little Phillida up in her strong young arms, and ran downstairs just in time to greet the boys as they dismounted at the door, and shake hands demurely with Lionel Young, who came with them. All three had raced down from the very top of the Upper Valley at breakneck speed, to be in time to welcome the travellers.

There is always one moment, big with fate, when processes begin to take place; when the first fine needle of crystallization forms in the transparent fluid; when the impulse of the jellying principle begins to work on the fruit-juice, and the frost principle to inform the water atoms. These fateful moments are not always perceptible to our dull apprehensions, but none the less do they exist; and they are apt to take us by surprise, because we have not detected the fine gradual chain of preparation which has made ready for them.

I think one of those fateful moments occurred that evening, as Lionel Young held Joanna Carr's hand, and his straightforward English eyes poured an ardent beam of welcome into hers. They had seen a good deal of each other two years before, but neither was prepared to be quite so glad to meet again. They did not pause to analyse or classify their feelings— people rarely do when they really feel; but from that night their attitude toward each other was changed, and the change became more apparent with every day that followed.

As these days went on, bright, golden days, cloudless, and full of the zest and snap of the nearing cold, Dorry grew stronger and stronger.

So well did he feel that after the first week or so he began to allude to himself as quite recovered, and to show an ominous desire to get back to his work; but this suggestion was promptly scouted by everybody, especially by John, who said she had come for six weeks at least, and six weeks at least she should stay—and as much longer as she could; and that Dorry as her escort must stay too, no matter how well he might feel.

'Besides,' she argued, 'there's all your life before you in which to dig away at dynamos and things, and you may never be in Colorado again. You wouldn't have the heart to disappoint Clover and Elsie and hurry back, when there's no real necessity. They are so pleased to have a visit from you.'

'Oh, I'll stay! I'll certainly stay,' said Dorry. 'You shall have your visit out, John; only, when a fellow feels as perfectly well as I do, it seems ridiculous for him to be sitting round with his hands folded, taking a mountain cure which he doesn't need.'

Autumn is the busiest season for cattlemen everywhere, which made it the more singular that Lionel Young should manage to find so much time for sitting and riding with Johnnie, or taking her to walk up the steepest and loneliest canyons. They were together in one way or another half the day at least; and during the other half Johnnie's face wore always a preoccupied look, and was dreamily happy and silent. Even Clover began to perceive that something unusual was in the air, something that seemed a great deal too good to be true. She and Elsie held conferences in private, during which they hugged each other, and whispered that 'If! Whenever—if ever! Papa would surely come out and live in the Valley. He never could resist three of his girls all at once.' But they resolved not to say one word to Johnnie, or even look as if they suspected anything, lest it should have a discouraging effect.

'It never does to poke your finger into a bird's nest,' observed Elsie, with a sapient shake of the head. 'The eggs always addle if you do, or the young birds refuse to hatch out; and of course in the case of turtle-doves it would be all the more so. "Lay low, Bre'r Fox," and wait for what happens. It all promises delightfully, only I don't see exactly, supposing this ever comes to anything, how Imogen Young is to be disposed of.'

'We won't cross that bridge till we come to it,' said Clover; but all the same she did cross it in her thoughts many times. It is not in human nature to keep off these mental bridges.

At the end of the fortnight Imogen returned in very good looks and spirits; and further beautified by a pretty autumn dress of dark blue, which Mrs. Hope had persuaded her to order, and over the making of which she herself had personally presided. It fitted well, and set off to admiration the delicate pink and white of Imogen's skin, while the new warmth of affection which had come into her manner was equally becoming.

'Why didn't you say what a pretty girl Miss Young was?' demanded Dorry the very first evening.

'I don't know, I'm sure. She looks better than she did before she was ill, and she's very nice and all that, but we never thought of her being exactly pretty.'

'I can't think why; she is certainly much better-looking than that Miss Chase who was here the other day. I should call her decidedly handsome; and she seems easy to get on with too.'

'Isn't it odd?' remarked Elsie, as she retailed this conversation to Clover. 'Imogen never seemed to me so very easy to get on with, and Dorry never before seemed to find it particularly easy to get on with any girl. I suppose they happen to suit, but it is very queer that they should. People are always surprising you in that way.'

What with John's recently developed tendency to disappear into canyons with Lionel Young, with the boys necessarily so occupied, and their own many little tasks and home duties, there had been moments during the fortnight when Clover and Elsie had found Dorry rather heavy on their hands. He was not much of a reader except in a professional way, and still less of a horseman; so the two principal amusements of the Valley counted for little with him, and they feared he would feel dull, or fancy himself neglected. With the return of Imogen these apprehensions were laid at rest. Dorry, if left alone, promptly took the trail in the direction of the 'Hutlet', returning hours after-ward looking beaming and contented, to mention casually by way of explanation that he had been reading aloud to Miss Young, or that he and Miss Young had been taking a walk.

'It's remarkably convenient,' Elsie remarked one evening; 'but it's just as remarkably queer. What can they find to say to each other, do you suppose?'

If Dorry had not been Dorry, besides being her brother, she would probably have arrived at a conclusion about the matter much sooner than she did. Quick people are too apt to imagine that slow people have nothing to say, or do not know how to say it when they have; while all the time, for slow and quick alike, there is the old, old story for each to tell in his own way, which makes the most halting lips momentarily eloquent, and which both to speaker and listener seems forever new, fresh, wonderful, and inexhaustibly interesting.

In a retired place like the High Valley intimacies flourish with wonderful facility and quickness. A month in such a place counts for more than half a year amid the confusions and interruptions of the city. Dorry had been struck by Imogen that first evening. He had never got on very well with girls, or known much about them; there was a delightful novelty in his present sensations. There was not a word as to the need of getting back to business after she dawned on his horizon. Quite the contrary. Two weeks, three, four went by; the original limit set for the visit was passed, the end of his holiday drew near, and still he stayed on contentedly, and every day devoted himself more and more to Imogen Young.

She, on her part, was puzzled and flattered, but not unhappy. She was quite alive to Dorry's merits; he was her first admirer, and it was a new and agreeable feature of life to have one, 'like other girls', as she told herself. Lionel was too much absorbed in his own affairs to notice or interfere; so the time went on, and the double entanglement wound itself naturally and happily to its inevitable conclusion.

It was in the beautiful little ravine to the east, which Clover had named 'Pentstemon Canyon', from the quantity of those flowers which grew there, that Dorry made his final declaration. There were no pentstemons in the valley now, no yuccas or columbines, only a few belated autumn crocuses and the scarlet berried mats of kinnikinnick remained; but the day was as golden-bright as though it were still September.

'We have known each other only four weeks,' said Dorry, going straight to the point in his usual direct fashion; 'and if I were going to stay on I should think I had no right, perhaps, to speak so soon—for your sake, mind, not for my own; I could not be surer about my feelings for you if we had been acquainted for years. But I have to go away before long, back to my home and my work, and I really cannot go without speaking. I must know if there is a chance for me.'

*I like you very much,' said Imogen, demurely. 'Do you? Then perhaps one day you might get to like me

better still. I'd do all that a man could to make you happy if you would, and I think you'd like Burnet to live in. It's a big place, you know, with all the modem improvements—not like this, which, pretty as it is, would be rather lonely in the winters, I should think. There are lots of nice people in Burnet, and there's Johnnie, whom you already know, and my father—you'd be sure to like my father.'

'Oh, don't go on in this way, as if it were only for the advantages of the change that I should consent. It would be for quite different reasons, if I did.' Then, after a short pause, she added, 'I wonder what they will say at Bideford.'

It was an indirect yes, but Dorry understood that it was yes.

'Then you'll think of it? You don't refuse me? Imogen, you make me very happy.'

Dorry did look happy; and as bliss is beautifying, he looked handsome as well. His strong, well-knit figure

showed to advantage in the rough climbing-suit which he wore; his eyes sparkled and beamed as he looked at Imogen.

'May I talk with Lionel about it?' he asked persuasively. 'He represents your father over here, you know.'

'Yes, I suppose so.' She blushed a little, but looked frankly up at Dorry. 'Poor Lion! It's hard lines for him, and I feel guilty at the idea of deserting him so soon; but I know your sisters will be good to him, and I can't help being glad that you care for me. Only there's one thing I must say to you, Theodore (no one since he was baptized had ever called Dorry "Theodore" till now!), for I don't want you to fancy me nicer than I really am. I was horribly stiff and prejudiced when I first came out. I thought everything American was inferior and mistaken, and all the English ways were best; and I was nasty—yes, really very nasty to your sisters, especially dear Clover. I have learned her worth now, and I love her and America, and I shall love it all the better for your sake; but all the same, I shall probably disappoint you sometimes, and be stiff and impracticable and provoking, and you will need to have patience with me; it's the price you must pay if you marry an English wife—this particular English wife, at least.'

'It's a price that I'll gladly pay,' cried Dorry, holding her hand tight. 'Not that I believe a word you say; but you are the dearest, truest, honestest girl in the world, and I love you all the better for being so modest about yourself. For me, I'm just a plain, sober sort of fellow. I never was bright like the others, and there's nothing in the least "subtle" or hard to understand about me; but I don't believe I shall make the worse husband for that. It's only in French novels that dark, inscrutable characters are good for daily use.'

'Indeed, I don't want an inscrutable husband. I like you much better as you are.' Then, after a happy pause, 'Isabel Templestowe—she's Geoff's sister, you know, and my most intimate friend at home— predicted that I should marry over here, but I never supposed I should. It didn't seem likely that anyone would want me, for I'm not pretty or interesting, like your sisters, you know.'

'Oh, I say!' cried Dorry, 'haven't I been telling you that you interest me more than anyone in the world ever did before? I never saw a girl whom I considered could hold a candle to you—certainly not one of my own sisters. You don't think your people at home will make any objections, do you?'

'No, indeed; they'll be very pleased to have me settled, I should think. There are a good many of us at home, you know.'

Meanwhile, a little farther up the same canyon, but screened from observation by a projecting shoulder of rock, another equally satisfactory conversation was going on between another pair of lovers. Johnnie and Lionel had strolled up there about an hour before Dorry and Imogen arrived. They had no idea that anyone else was in the ravine.

'I think I knew two years ago that I cared more for you than anyone else,' Lionel was saying.

'Did you? Perhaps the faintest suspicion of such a thing occurred to me too.'

'I used to keep thinking about you at odd minutes all day, when I was working over the cattle and everything, and I always thought steadily about you at night when I was falling asleep.'

'Very strange, certainly.'

'And the moment you came and I saw you again, it flashed upon me what it meant; and I perceived that 1 had been desperately in love with you all along without knowing it.'

'Still stranger.'

'Don't tease me, darling Johnnie—no, Joan; I like that better than Johnnie. It makes me think of Joan d'Arc. I shall call you that, may I?' 'How can I help it? You have a big will of your own, as I always knew, only don't connect me with the ark unless you spell it, and don't call me Jonah.'

'Never! He was the prophet of evil, and you are the good genius of my life.'

'I'm not sure whether I am or not. It plunges you into all sorts of embarrassments to think of marrying me. Neither of us has any money. You'll have to work hard for years before you can afford a wife—and then there's your sister to be considered.'

'I know. Poor Moggy! But she came out for my sake. She will probably be only too glad to get home again whenever other arrangements are possible. Will you wait a while for me, my sweet?'

'I don't mind if I do.'

'How long will you wait?'

'Shall we say ten years?'

'Ten years! By Jove, no! We'll say no such thing! But eighteen months—we'll fix it at eighteen months, or two years at farthest. I can surely fetch it in two years.'

'Very well, then; I'll wait two years with pleasure.'

'I don't ask you to wait with pleasure} That's carrying it a little too far!'

'I don't seem able to please you, whatever I say,' remarked Johnny, pretending to pout.

'Please me, darling Joan! You please me down to the ground, and you always did! But if you'll wait two years—not with pleasure, but with patience and resignation—I'll buckle to with a will and earn my happiness. Your father won't be averse, will he?'

'Poor Papa! Yes, he is very averse to having his girls marry, but he's somewhat hardened to it. I'm the last of the four, you know, and I think he would give his blessing to you rather than anyone else, because you would bring me out here to live near the others. Perhaps he will come too. It is the dream of Clover's and Elsie's lives that he should.'

'That would be quite perfect for us all.' 'You say that to please me, I know, but you will say it with all your heart if ever it happens, for my father is the sweetest man in the world, and the wisest and most reasonable. You will love him dearly. He has been father and mother and all to us children. And there's my sister Katy—you will love her too.'

'I have seen her once, you remember.' 'Yes; but you can't find Katy out at once— there is too much of her. Oh, I've ever so many nice relations to give you. There's Ned Worthington; he's a dear—and Cousin Helen. Did I ever tell you about her? She's a terrible invalid, you know, almost always confined to her bed or sofa, and yet she has been one of the great influences of our lives—a sort of guardian angel, always helping and brightening and cheering us all, and starting us in right directions. Oh, you must know her. I can't think how you ever will, for of course she can never come to Colorado; but somehow it shall be managed. Now tell me about your people. How many are there of you?'

'Eleven, and I scarcely remember my oldest brother, he went away from home so long ago. Jim was my chum—he's no end of a good fellow. He's in New Zealand now. And Beatrice—that's the next girl to Imogen—is awfully nice too, and there are one or two jolly ones among the smaller kids. Oh, you'll like them all, especially • my mother. We'll go over some day and make them a visit.'

'That will be nice; but we shall have to wait till we grow rich before we can take such a long journey. Lion, do you think by-and-by we could manage to build another house, or move your cabin farther down the Valley? I want to live nearer Clover and Elsie. You'll have to be away a good deal, of course, as the other boys are, and a mile is "a goodish bit", as Imogen would say. It would make all the difference in the world if I had the sisters close at hand to "put my lips to when so disposed".'

'Why, of course we will. Geoff built the Hutlet, you know; I didn't put any money into it. I chose the position because—well, the view was so good, and I didn't know how Moggy would hit it off with the rest, you understand. I thought she might do better a little farther away; but with you it's quite different of course. I dare say the Hutlet could be moved; I'll talk to Geoff about it.'

'I don't care how simple it is, so long as it is near the others,' went on Johnnie. 'It's easy enough to make a simple house pretty and nice. I am so glad that your house is in this valley, Lion.' • A little pause ensued.

'What was that?' asked Johnnie suddenly.

'What?'

'That sound? It seemed to come from down the canyon. Such a very odd echo, if it was an echo!'

'What kind of a sound? I heard nothing.'

'Voices, I should say, if it were not quite impossible that it could be voices—very low and hushed, as if a ghost were confabulating with another ghost about a quarter of a mile away.'

'Oh, that must be just a fancy,' protested Lionel. 'There isn't a living soul within a mile of us.'

And at the same moment, Dorry, a couple of hundred feet distant, was remarking to Imogen;

'These canyons do have the most extraordinary echoes.

There's the strangest cooing and sibilating going on above.'

'Wood pigeons, most probably; there are heaps of them hereabout.'

Presently the pair from above, slowly climbing down the ravine hand-in-hand, came upon the pair below, just rising from their seat to go home. There was a mutual consternation in the four countenances comical to behold.

'You here!' cried Imogen.

'And you here!' retorted Lionel. 'Why, we never suspected it. What brought you up?—and Carr, too, I declare!'

'Why—oh—it's a pretty place,' stammered Imogen.

'Theodore—Mr. Carr, I mean—now, Lionel, what are you laughing at?'

'Nothing,' said her brother, composing his features as best he could; 'only it's such a very odd coincidence, you know.'

'Very odd indeed,' remarked Dorry, gravely. The four looked at one another solemnly and questioningly, and then—it was impossible to help it—all four laughed.

'By Jove!' cried Lionel, between his paroxysms, 'I do believe we have come up here on the same errand!'

'I dare say we have,' remarked Dorry; 'there were some extremely queer echoes that came down to us from above.'

'Not a bit queerer, I assure you, than some which floated up to us from below,' retorted Johnnie, recovering her powers of speech.

'We thought it was doves.'

'And we were sure it was ghosts—affectionate ghosts, you know, on excellent terms with each other.'

'Young, I want a word with you,' said Dorry, drawing Lionel aside.

'And I want a word with you.'

'And I want several words with you,' cried Johhnie, brightly, putting her arm through Imogen's. She looked searchingly at her.

'I'm going to be your sister,' she said; 'I've promised Lionel. Are you going to be mine?'

'Yes—I've promised Theodore— —'

'Theodore!' cried Johnnie, with a world of admiration in her voice. 'Oh, you mean Dorry. We never call him that, you know.'

'Yes, I know, but I prefer Theodore. Dorry seems a childish sort of name for a grown man. Do you mean to say that you are coming out to the Valley to live?'

'Yes, by-and-by, and you will come to Burnet; we shall just change places. Isn't it nice and queer?'

'It is a sort of double-barrelled International Alliance,' declared Lionel. 'Now let us go down and astonish the others.'

The others were astonished indeed. They were prepared for Johnnie's confession, but had so little thought of Dorry's that for some time he and Imogen stood by unheeded, waiting their turn at explanation.

'Why, Dorry,' cried Elsie at last, 'why are you standing on one side like that with Miss Young? You don't look as surprised as you ought. Did you hear the news before we did? Imogen dear—it isn't such good news for you as for us.'

'Oh, yes, indeed it is. I am quite as happy in it as you can be.'

'Ladies and gentlemen,' cried Lionel, who was in topping spirits and could not be restrained, 'this shrinking pair also have a tale to tell. It is a case of "change partners all round and down the middle". Let me introduce to you Mr. and Mrs. Theo——'

'Lion, you wretched boy, stop!' interrupted Johnnie. 'That's not at all the right way to do it. Let me introduce them. Friends and countrymen, allow the echoes of the Upper East Canyon to present to your favourable consideration the echoes of the Lower East Canyon. We've all been sitting up there, "unbeknownst", within a few feet of each other, and none of us could account for the mysterious noises that we heard, till we all started to come home, and met each other on the way down.'

'What kind of noises?' demanded Elsie, in a suffocated voice.

'Oh, cooings and gurglings and soft murmurs of conversation and whisperings. It was very unaccountable indeed, very!' 'Dorry,' said Elsie, next day when she chanced to be alone with him, 'would you mind if I asked you rather an impertinent question? You needn't answer if you don't want to; but what was it that first put it into your head to fall in love with Imogen Young? I'm very glad that you did, you understand. She will make you a capital wife, and I'm going to be very fond of her—but still, I should just like to know.'

'I don't know that I could tell you if I tried,' replied her brother. 'How can a man explain that sort of thing? I fell in love because I was destined to fall in love, I suppose. I liked her at the start, and thought her pretty, and all that; and she seemed kind of lonely and left out among you all. And then she's a quiet sort of girl, you know, not so ready at talk as most, or so quick to pick at a fellow or trip him up. I've always been the slow one in our family, you see, and by way of a change it's rather refreshing to be with a woman who isn't so much brighter than I am. The rest of you jump at an idea and off it again while I'm gathering my wits together to see that there is an idea. Imogen doesn't do that, and it rather suits me that she shouldn't. You're all delightful, and I'm very fond of you, I'm sure; but for a wife I think I like someone more like myself.'

'Of all the droll explanations that I ever heard, that is quite the drollest,' said Elsie to her husband afterward. 'The idea of a man's falling in love with a woman because she's duller than his own sisters! Nobody but Dorry would ever have thought of it.'

CHAPTER TEN: A DOUBLE KNOT

The next few days in the High Valley were too full of excitement and discussions to be quite comfortable for anybody. Imogen was seized with compunctions at leaving Lionel without a housekeeper, and proposed to Dorry that their wedding should be deferred till the others were ready to be married also—a suggestion to which Dorry would not listen for a moment. There were long business-talks between the ranch partners as to hows and whens, letters to be written, and innumerable confabulations between the three sisters, in which Imogen took part, for she counted as a fourth sister now. Clover and Elsie listened and planned and advised, and found their chief difficulty to consist in hiding and keeping in the background their unfeigned and flattering joy over the whole arrangement. It made matters so delightfully easy all round to have Imogen engaged to Dorry, and it was so much to their own individual advantage to exchange her for Johnnie that they really dared not express their delight too openly. The great question with all was how Papa would take the announcement and whether he could be induced to carry out his half promise of leaving Burnet and coming to live with them in the Valley. They waited anxiously for his reply to the letters. It came by telegraph two days before they had dared to hope for it, and was as follows:

God bless you all four! Genesis XLIII, 14.

P. CARR.

This Biblical addition nearly broke John's heart. Her sisters had to comfort her with all manner of hopeful auguries and promises.

'He'll be glad enough over it in time,' they told her. 'Think what it would have been if you had been going to marry a Californian, or a man with an orange plantation in Florida. He'll see that it's all for the best as soon as he gets out here, and he must come. Johnnie, you must never let him off. Don't take "no" for an answer. It is so important to us all that he should consent.'

They primed her with persuasive messages and arguments, and both Clover and Elsie wrote him a long letter on the subject. On the very eve of the departure came a second telegram. Telegrams were not everyday things in the High Valley, the nearest 'wire' being at the Ute Hotel five miles away; and the arrival of the messenger on horseback created a momentary panic.

This telegram was also from Dr. Carr. It was addressed to Johnnie:

Following just received: 'Miss Inches died today of

pneumonia.' No particulars.

P. CARR.

It was a great shock to poor Johnnie. She and 'Mamma Marian', as she still called her godmother, had been warm friends always; they corresponded regularly; Johnnie had made her several long visits at Inches Mills, and she had written to her among the first with the news of her engagement.

'She never got it. She never will know about Lionel,' she kept repeating mournfully. 'And now I can never tell her about any of my plans, and she would have been so pleased and interested. She always cared so much for what I cared about, and I hoped she would come out here for a long visit some day, and see you all.

Oh dear, oh dear! What a sad ending to our happy time!'

'Not an ending, only an interruption,' put in the comforting Clover. But John for a time could not be consoled, and the party broke up under a cloud, literal as well as metaphorical, for the first snowstorm was drifting over the plain as they drove down the pass, the melting flakes instantly drunk in by the sand; all the soft blue of distance had vanished, and a grey mist wrapped the mountain tops. The High Valley was in temporary eclipse, its brightness and sparkle put by for the moment.

But nothing could long eclipse the sunshine of such youthful hearts and hopes. Before long John's letters grew cheerful again, and presently she wrote to announce a wonderful piece of news.

'Something very strange has happened,' she began. 'I am an heiress! It is just like the girls in books! Yesterday came a letter from a firm of lawyers in Boston with a long document enclosed. It was an extract from Mamma Marian's will; and only think—she has left me a legacy of thirty thousand dollars! Dear thing! And she never knew about my engagement either, or how wonderfully it was going to help in our plans. She just did it because she loved me. "To Joanna Inches Carr, my namesake and child by affection", the will says; and I think it pleases me as much as having the money. That frightens me a little, it seems so much. At first I did not like to take it, and felt as if I might be robbing someone else; but Papa says that she had no very near relatives, and that I need not hesitate. Oh, my darling Clover, is it not wonderful? Now Lion and I need not wait two years, unless he prefers it, and can just go on and make our plans happily to suit ourselves and all of you—and I shall love to think that we owe it all to dear Mamma Marian; only it will be a sore spot always that she never got the letter telling of our engagement. It came just after she died, and they returned it to me.

'Ned has his orders at last. He goes to sea in April, and Katy writes to Papa that she will come and spend a year with him if he likes, while Ned is away. But Papa won't be here. He has quite decided, I think, to leave Burnet and make his home for the future with us in the High Valley. Three different physicians have already offered to buy out his practice, and it is arranged that Dorry shall rent the old house of his, and the furniture too, except the books and a few special things which Papa wishes to keep. He is going to write to you about the building of what he is pleased to call "a separate shanty"; but please don't let the shanty be really separate; he must be in with all of us somehow, or we shall never be satisfied. Did Lionel decide to move the Hutlet? Of course Katy will spend her year in the Valley instead of Burnet. I am beginning to get my little trousseau together, and have set up a "wedding bureau" to put the things in; but it is no fun at all without any sisters at home to help and sympathize. I am the only one who has had to get ready to be married all by herself. If Katy were not coming in two months I should be quite desperate. The chief thing on my mind is how to arrange about the two weddings with the family so scattered as it is.'

This difficulty was settled by Clover a little later. Both the weddings she proposed should take place in the Valley.

'It is a case of Mahomet and mountain,' she wrote. 'Look at it dispassionately. You and Papa and Katy and Dorry have got to come out here anyway—the rest of us are here; and it is clearly impossible that all of us should go on to Burnet to see you married—though if you persist some of us will, inconvenient and expensive as it would be. But just consider what a picturesque and romantic place the Valley is for a wedding, with the added advantage that you would be absolutely the first people who were ever married in it since the creation of the world! I won't say what may happen in the remote future, for Rose Red writes that she is going to change its name and call it henceforward "The Ararat Valley", not only because it contains "a few souls, that is eight", but also because all the creatures who go into it seem to enter pell-mell and come out two by two in pairs. You will inaugurate the long procession at all events! Do please think seriously of this, dear John. "Consider, cow, consider——-" and write me that you consent.

'We are building Papa the most charming little bungalow ever seen—a big library and two bedrooms, one for himself and one to spare. It is just off the southwest comer, and a little covered way connects it with our piazza; for we are quite decided that he is to take his meals with us and not have the bother of independent housekeeping. Then if you decide to put your bungalow on the other side of his, as we hope you will, we shall all be close together. Lion will do nothing about the building till you come. You are to stay on indefinitely with us, and oversee the whole thing yourself from the driving of the first nail. We will all help, and won't it be fun?

'There is something very stately and comforting in the idea of a "resident physician". Elsie declares that now Phillida may have croup or any other infant disease she likes, and I shan't lie awake at night to wonder what we should do in case Geoffrey was thrown from the burro and broke a bone. I am not sure but we may yet attain to the dignity of a "resident pastor" as well, for Geoff has decided not to move the Hutlet, but leave it as it is, putting in a little simple furniture, and offer it from time to time to some invalided clergyman who needs Colorado air and would be glad to spend a few months in the Valley. Who knows but it may grow some day into a little church? Then indeed we should have a small world of our own, with the learned professions all represented; for of course Phil by that time will be qualified to do our law for us, in case we quarrel and require writs and replevins or habeas corpuses, or any last wills and testaments drawn up.

'I have begun on new curtains for Katy's room already, and Elsie and I have all manner of beautiful projects for the weddings. Now Johnnie darling, write at once and say that you agree to this plan. It really does seem a perfect one for everybody. The time must of course depend on when Dorry can get his leave, but we will be all ready whenever it comes.'

Clover's arguments were unanswerable, and everyone gradually gave in to the plan which she had so much at heart. Dorry got a fortnight's holiday, beginning on the 15th of June; so the twentieth was fixed as the day for the double wedding, and the preparations went merrily on. Early in May Katy arrived in Burnet; and after that Johnnie had no need to complain of being unsistered, for Katy was a host in herself, and gave all her time to helping everybody. She sewed and finished, she packed and advised, she assisted to box her father's books, and went with Dorry to choose the new papers and rugs which were to make the old house freshly bright for Imogen; she exclaimed and rejoiced over each wedding present that arrived, and supplied that sweet atmosphere of mutual interest and sympathy which is the vital breath of a family occasion. All was ready in time; the old home was in exact and perfect order for its new mistress, the good-byes were said, and on the morning of the fifteenth the party started for Colorado.

Quite a little group waited for them on the platform of the St. Helen's station three days later. Lionel had of course come in to meet his bride, and Imogen her bridegroom; and Geoff had come, and Clover, to meet her father and Katy, and Phil was also in waiting. It was truly a wonderful moment when the train drew up;, and Johnnie, all beautiful in smiles and dimples^ encountered Lionel; while Dorry jumped out to greet Imogen, who was in blooming health again, and very pleased to see him.

'We have brought the two carry-alls,' Clover explained. 'Geoff got a new one the other day, that the means of transportation may keep pace with the increase of population, as he says. I think, Geoff, we will put the brides and bridegrooms together in the new one. Then the "echoes" from the back seat can mix with the "echoes" from the front seat; and it will be as good as the East Canyon, and they will all feel at home.'

So it was arranged, and the party started.

'Katy,' cried Clover, looking at her sister with eyes that seemed to drink her in, 'I had forgotten quite how dear you are! It seems to me that you have grown handsome, my child; or is it only that you are a little fatter?'

'I am afraid the latter,' replied Katy, with a laugh. 'No one but Ned was ever so deluded as to call me handsome.'

'Where is Ned? It is such a shame that he can't be here—the only one of the family missing!'

'He is on his way to China,' said Katy, with a little suppressed sigh. 'Yes, it is too bad; but it can't be helped. Naval orders are like time and tide, and wait for no man, and most of all for no woman.' She paused a moment, and changed the subject abruptly. 'Did I tell you,' she asked, 'that after I broke up at Newport I went to Rose for a week?'

'Johnnie wrote that you were to go.'

'It was such a bright week! Boston was beautiful, as it always is in spring, with the Public Garden a blaze of flowers, and all the pretty country about so green and sweet! Rose was most delightful; and I saw ever so many of the old Hillsover girls, and even had a glimpse of Mrs. Nipson!'

'That must have been rather a bad joy.'

'N-o, not exactly. I was rather glad, on the whole, to meet her again. She isn't as bad as we made her out. Schoolgirls are almost always unjust to their teachers.'

'Oh, come, now,' said Clover, making a little face. 'This is a happy occasion, certainly, and I am in a benignant frame of mind, but really I can't stand having you so horridly charitable. "There is no virtue, madam, in a mush of concession." Mrs. Nipson was an unpleasant old thing—so there! Let us talk of something else. Tell me about your visit to Cousin Helen.'

'Oh, that was a sweet visit all through. I stayed ten days, and she was better than usual, it seemed to me. Did I write about little Helen's ball?' :

'No.'

'She is just nineteen, and it was her first dance. Such a pretty creature, and so pleased and excited about it! And Cousin Helen was equally so. She gave Helen her dress complete down to the satin shoes, and the fan and the long gloves, and a turquoise necklace, and turquoise pins for her hair. You never saw anything so charming as the way in which she enjoyed it. You would have supposed that Helen was her own child, as she lay on the sofa, with such bright beaming eyes, while the pretty thing turned round and round and round to exhibit her finery.'

'There certainly never was anyone like Cousin Helen. She is embodied sympathy,' said Clover. 'Now, Katy, I want you to look. We are just turning into our own road.'

It was a radiant afternoon, with long, soft shadows alternating with golden sunshine, and the High Valley was at its very best, as they slowly climbed the zigzag pass. With every turn and winding Katy's pleasure grew; and when they rounded the last curve, and came in sight of the little group of buildings, with their picturesque background of forest and the splendid peak soaring above, she exclaimed with delight:

'What a perfect situation! Clover, you never .said enough about it! Surely the half was not told me, as the Queen of Sheba remarked! Oh, and there is Elsie on the porch, and that thing in white beside her is PhilUda! I never dreamed she could be so large! How glad I am that I didn't die of measles when I was little, as dear Red Rose used to say.'

Katy's coming was the crowning pleasure of the occasion to all, but most of all to Clover. To have her most intimate sister in her own home, and be able to see her every day and all day long, and consult and advise and lay before her the hopes and intentions and desires of her heart, which she could never so fully share with anyone else, except Geoff, was a delight which never lost its zest, and of which Clover never grew weary.

To settle Dr.- Can- in his new quarters was another pleasure, in which they all took equal part. When his books and microscopes were unpacked, and the Burnet belongings arranged pretty much in their old order, the rooms looked wonderfully homelike, even to him. The children soon learned to adore him, as children always had done; the only trouble was that they fought for the possession of his knee, and would never willingly have left him a moment for himself. His leisure had to be protected by a series of nursery laws and penances, or he would never have had any; but he said he liked the children better than the leisure. He was born to be a grandfather; nobody told stories like him, or knew so well how to please and pacify and hit the taste of little people.

But all this, of course, came subsequently to the double wedding, which took place two days after the arrival of the home-party. The morning of the twentieth was unusually fine, even for Colorado—fair, cloudless, and golden bright, as if ordered for the occasion—without a cloud in the sky from dawn to sunset. The ceremony was performed by a clergyman from Portland. He and his invalid wife were settled in the Hutlet for the summer, very glad of the pleasant little home offered them, and to escape from the crowd and confusion of Mrs. Marsh's boarding-house, where Geoff had found them. Two or three particular friends drove out from St. Helen's; but with that exception the whole wedding was 'valley-made', as Elsie declared, including delicious raspberry ice-cream, and an enormous cake, over which she and Clover had expended much time and thought, and which, decorated with emblematical designs in icing and wreathed yucca-blossoms, stood in the middle of the table.

The ceremony took place at noon precisely, when, as Phil facetiously observed, 'the shadows of the high contracting parties could never be less'. There was little that was formal about it, but much that was reverent and sweet and full of true feeling. Imogen and Johnnie had both agreed to wear white muslin dresses, very much such dresses as they were all accustomed to wear on afternoons; but Imogen had on her head her mother's wedding-veil, which had been sent out from England, and John wore Katy's, 'for luck', as she said. Both carried a big bouquet of Mariposa lilies, and the house was filled with the characteristic wild-flowers of the region most skilfully and effectively grouped and arranged.

A hospitably hearty luncheon followed the ceremony, of which all partook; then Imogen went away to put on her pretty travelling suit of pale brown, and the carry-all came round to take Mr. and Mrs. Theodore Carr to St. Helen's, which was the first stage on their journey of life.

The whole party stood on the porch to see them go. Imogen's last word and embrace were for Clover.

'We are sisters now,' she whispered. 'I belong to you just as much as Isabel does, and I am so glad that I do! Dear Clover, you have been more good to me than I can say, and I shall never forget it.'

'Nonsense about being good! You are my Dorry's wife now, and our own dear sister. There is no question about goodness—only to love one another.'

She kissed Imogen warmly, and helped her into the carriage. Dorry sprang after her; the wheels revolved; and Phil, seizing a horseshoe which hung ready to hand on the wall of the house, flung it after the departing vehicle.

'It's more appropriate than any other sort of old shoe for this Place of Hoofs,' he observed. 'Well, the Carr family are certainly pretty well disposed of now. I am "the last ungathered rose on my ancestral tree". I wonder who will tear me from my stem!'

'You can afford to hang on a while longer,' remarked Elsie. 'I don't consider you fairly expanded yet, by any means. You'll be twice as well worth gathering a few years from now.'

'Oh, very fine!—years indeed! Why, I shall be a seedy old bachelor! That would never do! And Amy Ashe, whom I have had in my eye ever since she was in pinafores, will be married to some other fellow!'

'Don't set your heart on Amy,' said Katy. 'She's not seventeen yet; and I don't think her mother has any idea of having her made into Ashe-s of Roses so early!'

'There's no harm in having a girl in one's eye,' retorted Phil, disconsolately. 'I declare, you all look so contented and so satisfied with yourselves and one another, that it's enough to madden a fellow, left out, as I am, in the cold! I shall go back to St. Helen's with Dr. and Mrs. Hope.'

The others, left to themselves in their happy loneliness, gathered together in the big room after the last guest had gone. Geoff touched a match to the ready-laid fire; Clover wheeled an armchair forward for her father, and sat down beside him with her arm on his knee; John and Lionel took possession of a big sofa.

'Now let us enjoy ourselves,' said Clover.

'The world is shut out, we are shut in; there are none to molest and make us afraid; and, please Heaven, there is a whole, long, happy year before us! I never did suppose anything so perfectly perfect could happen to us all as this. Now, Papa—dear Papa—just say that you like it as much as we all do.'

Elsie perched herself on the arm of her father's chair; Katy stood behind, stroking his hair. Dr. Carr held out his hand to Johnnie, who ran across the room, knelt down, caught it in both hers, and fondly laid her cheek upon it.

'I like it quite as much as you do,' he said. 'Where my girls are is the place for me; and I am going to be the most contented old gentleman in America for the rest of my days.'